WRITTEN ON THE WIND

Lynn Granger

CHIVERS

British Library Cataloguing in Publication Data available

This Large Print edition published by BBC Audiobooks Ltd, Bath, 2008.
Published by arrangement with the Author.

U.K. Hardcover ISBN 978 1 405 64318 4
U.K. Softcover ISBN 978 1 405 64319 1

Printed and bound in Great Britain by
Antony Rowe Ltd., Chippenham, Wiltshire

CHAPTER ONE

Sheana Lyon stretched her arms high, relishing the 'good to be alive' feeling after an early morning swim. The waters of the Solway Firth were cold but Sheana loved the exhilarating tingle of blood coursing through her veins as she towelled herself dry and scrambled into her jeans and sweatshirt. Then she remembered the plans for the caravan site. She sighed and her joy evaporated. There was no other option. She had thought of plans, and rejected them, until her brain reeled.

The idea of diversifying into caravans was borne of desperation. It was the only way she could think of to keep Creagbowie for Tommy, her young brother. It was his home, his heritage, but the farm was too small to carry on as a viable business, especially now, without their father. She sighed again, her heart heavy.

Once the plans were passed, the caravan site would be situated further along the shore, around the curve of the headland. It would not be visible from this tiny bay which Sheana had always regarded as her special place, but the tourists would have to use the farm track to reach it and that meant they would traverse across her little cove.

She shielded her eyes with her hand against the bright rays of the morning sun and drank in the view of the glittering waves as they raced towards the shore, with the Galloway hills outlined against the western sky and the peak of Skiddaw and the Cumberland Fells to the east.

She stiffened. Against the red and gold horizon of the rising sun she glimpsed the figure of a man. He was lost to view behind a grassy mound. When he appeared again, jogging along the newly washed sand, he was only fifty yards away. He looked up and saw her. He waved and called a greeting.

'It seems I'm not the only early bird!' he grinned as he drew to a halt. 'You've been swimming?' His eyes widened as he took in her long damp hair and the swimsuit and towel dangling from her hand. 'I thought the water would be too cold this early in the year?'

'It is rather, but the tide goes so far out you have to seize the opportunity whenever it's in at a convenient time. Anyway I'm used to it,' Sheana smiled back, unable to resist his infectious grin. He reminded her of a schoolboy playing truant. 'Are you on holiday?'

'No. Unfortunately.' He sighed. 'Just a quick business trip. I stayed at the hotel back there last night. I must return to London as soon as I've had breakfast. It's not ready yet so I couldn't resist taking an early morning walk.' His smile lit his eyes and Sheana knew instinctively that he shared her enjoyment of the fresh morning air and the world which had

2

barely begun to waken.

'I'd say it's more of a run.'

'Yes, well with air like wine it makes me feel I could run for ever . . .'

'You'd come to a sorry end,' Sheana grinned, 'swallowed up by the sea, or cast up on rocks somewhere.'

'Yes, I suppose so.' He smiled back at her, admiring her fresh, clear skin and unadorned hair, her long legs and slender figure. Everything about her was so natural, so unlike the sophisticated women he met every day. He wished he had allowed himself more time for this trip to Scotland. But it had been a spur of the moment thing, a sentimental whim, totally out of character for the man who was Managing Director of the A. & D. F. Development Company. 'Do you live round here?' he asked.

'I do now—since I returned home . . .' A tiny frown creased Sheana's brow and the laughter died from her bright gaze. She remembered the small herd of cows she was supposed to be collecting from their field for milking, and Tommy, her invalid brother, wafting patiently for her to return to the house to help him dress and do his exercises.

'I must go,' Sheana said, astonished that she felt so reluctant to leave the smiling stranger. It felt like leaving a good book before you discovered the ending.

'My name is Dean. I hope we'll meet again

. . .' the man said hurriedly.

Sheana gave him a fleeting smile of farewell. There was no point in lingering, however much she longed to know more about the man. She had already discovered her new responsibilities were not conducive to a satisfactory relationship—even with the man who had once pleaded with her to marry him. She shivered, thankful she had found out in time.

*   *   *

Charlene Dee-Smythe reached across the desk and picked up the telephone, stretching her slender wrist to admire the new gold bracelet. She punched in the number which would put her straight through to the Managing Director of A. & D. F. Developments, but it was the calm voice of Miss Pringle who answered. Charlene seethed.

'Put Dean on. I want to speak to him personally.' She made no pretence at preliminary greetings to the elderly private secretary. Miss Pringle had been with the company from its humble Scottish beginnings. She was an essential cog in the ever increasing wheels of the business, much to the chagrin of Charlene, who intended to be nothing less than Mrs Dean Fawcette, and possibly even Lady Fawcette in due course, if Dean would only permit her to use her own methods of

4

influencing the right people.

'I'm afraid Mr Fawcette is in a meeting, Miss Smith. He returned your e-mail and left instructions that he would check your reply this evening before he dines with Sir Rodney.'

'My name is Miss *Dee-Smythe*. As in scythe. How many more times must I tell you! This Scottish dump is preposterous! I can't imagine why he's interested in anything so far north. Tell him from me, there's a large fly in the ointment.'

'I did tell him the neighbouring farmer is proposing to expand his caravan site. He said you were er . . .' Miss Pringle mentally edited her boss's exact words, and chewed her lower lip, as she had done earlier in an effort not to return Dean's roguish smile. 'You will see his reply when you check your e-mails. Goodbye Miss Smith.' Charlene heard the click at the other end and slammed the receiver down with a most unladylike expletive.

She stared around the dark panelled room she had selected as her office at Fingaeli. She would never have insisted on coming to Scotland if she hadn't believed Dean was coming too. She had understood this latest project was dear to his heart, being north of the border, albeit only just across the Solway Firth.

Too late, she realised she should have listened to the cleaning woman and chosen one of the smaller rooms facing south west.

Instead she had brushed aside Mrs McCracken's advice and insisted on having the huge desk moved into his room with its high ceiling and chandelier.

It had taken three men from the village to manoeuvre the furniture out and the desk in. She had ignored their muttered protests and grunts of disapproval. Now she looked out of the long windows which faced north. There was little sun to bring either warmth or cheer until late evening and she had no intention of spending her evenings in the office.

Through the overgrown shrubs she caught glimpses of the lane which ran close to Fingaeli boundary fence. That was one thing she would see changed without delay she decided, compressing her lips into a disapproving line as she heard the chug-chug of an ancient tractor.

This was the second time in an hour it had gone towards the shore, heading for the proposed caravan park. The rickety trailer was piled high with fence posts and wire and the boy looked far too young to be driving such a dangerous contraption. Charlene peered closer. She had a glimpse of clear skin and a slender neck. Surely even a country lad wouldn't be seen dead in that ridiculous tammy.

Her frown deepened. She had gleaned what information she could about the neighbour whose boundary marched with Fingaeli, but she could get nothing out of the tight lipped Mrs McCracken. Charlene's mouth tightened. It was unthinkable that the caravan project should ever come to fruition so close to Fingaeli. She moved over to the computer and switched on to check the e-mails.

Sure enough there was one from Dean, brief and to the point as she had come to expect of a man who could organise the demolition of acres of steel and concrete with the speed of lightning, and still make his fortune from selling everything which could be salvaged.

Charlene frowned again as she considered Fingaeli House, the rambling building on the edge of the Solway, with its overgrown orchards and shrubbery. It was in stark contrast to any other project he had undertaken since Charlene had begun work for him three years earlier. She read his message.

A mere fly! No doubt you will swat it with your usual ruthless efficiency, but tread carefully. Fingaeli is of personal importance.

Charlene allowed herself a satisfied smile. She took his words as a compliment to her own efficiency. Dean Fawcette knew she could deal with any problem, but she had intended to have him join her for the weekend. She couldn't help wondering why this project held particular significance. She scanned the list of useful local contacts in front of her, and reached once more for the telephone.

It was lunch time when Sheana Lyon drove the tractor back to Creagbowie Farm. She recognised the green Astra immediately. Mike Bain was the planning officer assigned to this area. He had dealt with the plans she had submitted for the caravan site and her proposal had gone through without a hitch. As she jumped down from the tractor he strode towards her.

'What's wrong, Mike?' she asked. 'You look—anxious . . . ?'

'I've come to warn you. The chief told me less than an hour ago. Someone has put in an objection to your plans. Literally at the eleventh hour . . .'

'But why? I mean who would want to object?' Sheana asked in consternation. 'And why wait until the last minute?'

'I'm not sure yet. I've an inkling it may have something to do with Councillor Cobber though.'

'Councillor Cobber? He's the representative for this area, as well as being on the planning committee. He was all in favour of us extending the caravan site. He thought it would bring more trade to the area, and maybe more employment . . .'

'I wonder what sort of backhander he had in mind for his support,' Mike muttered cynically.

'Backhander . . . ?' Sheana frowned in bewilderment. Then her eyes widened. 'You're not serious!'

'Dunno. I do wonder about him sometimes . . .'

'He did mention getting a free holiday for his parents once a year, but he laughed. I thought he was joking . . .'

'Mmm . . .' Mike mused. 'I wouldn't be so sure.' He'd heard various stories about Cobber changing horses in mid-stream when offered a bonus.

He looked at Sheana's anxious face, her grey eyes wide and clear and full of integrity. She was one of the nicest, kindest girls he'd ever met, and he'd known a few before he married Jenny, an old school friend of Sheana's. He didn't believe any of them would have given up a promising career to take care of an orphaned half-brother, especially when Tommy might be crippled for the rest of his life. The accident, which had killed his mother and father, had been horrific by all accounts.

'I'll keep you informed,' he promised, 'but it will probably mean postponing the opening.' He decided not to mention his suspicions about the involvement of the company which had recently bought Fingaeli House and grounds. They were the only newcomers to the area and it was their property which would be most affected by caravans driving down the lane.

Most of the village people welcomed the idea of a tastefully landscaped caravan park down by the shore. The number of stands would be limited and there would be public access to a walk through the little woodland and pond which Sheana planned to create as the development progressed and when funds allowed. All she wanted was to make the farm into a viable business and to maintain a home for her young brother and her Aunt Ellie.

'Aunt Ellie will have seen your car from the kitchen window, Mike. She'll be laying an extra place. It's only soup and rolls at midday, but you know you're welcome. I want to get back to the fencing as soon . . .' She stopped and frowned. 'There'll not be any hurry if we can't open the site. We'll not mention the reason for your visit to Aunt Ellie, not yet anyway,' she pleaded.

'All right, but I hate to see you carrying all this responsibility yourself. How is Tommy doing?'

'Oh the new physiotherapist was really good with him. I'm sure he'll be walking again soon. It's the psychological effects I'm beginning to dread. He's petrified whenever I tell him we're going in the car, and he'll not go with anyone else but me, not even Aunt Ellie.'

'That's a pity. You can't do everything yourself.'

'Old Mr Kerr is lending a hand. He used to do fencing for the estate. He had to go home at eleven today, but he'll be back tomorrow . . .' She stopped and stared at Mike. 'But what

10

point is there? I—I can't believe anyone would go against us. Everyone in the village knows we're desperate to keep Creagbowie.

'It's Tommy's home for goodness sake. It's Great Aunt Ellie's too. She was born here. I won't let them stop us, Mike!' She raised her small chin defiantly and yanked off her tammy. Her long straight hair fell to her shoulders in a shining curtain of pale auburn.

'We shall keep on with the fencing,' she declared, 'and get everything ready, as we planned. The advertisements are already booked to welcome summer visitors. We can't afford to delay.'

Mike nodded unhappily as he followed her into the large sunny kitchen of Creagbowie. Rocks of yellow Sheana had told him the name meant, the morning she had showed him the site.

'But the rocks have worn away to golden sand and I reckon,' she had grinned. 'Now we have our own lovely sheltered bay, the sand and the sea.' She had stretched her arms high and wide and her long hair had streamed behind her, 'and there's the hills standing guard. What more could anyone want . . . ?'

'Nothing,' he had murmured then, watching her pirouette along the rippling, newly washed shore. She had told him of the good news they'd had that morning.

'We've just heard the surgeon says it's worth a chance to operate on Tommy to try and save

11

the sight of his other eye. We have to wait until he considers the time is right, but after so much bad news, well . . . it's just so wonderful.'

She had lifted her head with a determined tilt then, just as she was doing now. 'He's only a little boy and he's lost so much already. I'm sure the caravan site will bring in enough income to make Creagbowie profitable.'

'I don't see any problem,' he had told her cheerfully then, but that was before Fingaeli House had been bought by a development company.

CHAPTER TWO

Eleanor Lyon had been born to elderly parents twelve years after they believed their family was complete. Consequently she had been closer in age to her eldest nephew, Robert Lyon, Sheana's father.

Eleanor had completed her nursing training with the highest honours, then taken a job as nurse on a luxury liner. For three years she had revelled in discovering new places, but her joy had trebled when she fell in love with a young naval officer.

Eighteen months later they had become engaged and planned to marry when their ship returned to England. Just a week before they docked her virile young naval officer became gravely ill. Back on shore blood tests confirmed the fears of the ship's doctor. Eleanor nursed him devotedly for the final six months of his young life.

Later she learned that he had left her all he possessed—not a fortune, but a substantial insurance as well as the small house inherited from his parents. Wisely invested they now provided Ellie with a small monthly allowance. Unable to contemplate the life at sea without her beloved Iain, she had returned to hospital nursing, but not for long.

Her elderly father needed her care and she had given it willingly. Afterwards she returned to her work in hospital until Sheana's mother died with meningitis at the age of twenty-four. Ellie had moved back to Creagbowie, the house where she had been born and devoted herself to caring for her nephew and his baby daughter.

Never once had Sheana heard her great aunt grumble at the demands life had made on her. Her sweet serene smile was rarely absent and her unfailing love had given Sheana the security of an idyllically happy childhood.

It had been a surprise to everyone when seventeen years later, Robert Lyon married again, a young woman only twelve years older than Sheana. Angelina possessed considerable musical talent, but she had given up her career to marry Robert. She had urged Ellie to stay on at the little farm so that she could teach

13

music at local secondary schools.

Sheana herself had felt no resentment, indeed her life had been enriched. Angelina had treated her like a younger sister, with warmth and affection, helping her overcome her teenage uncertainties, and preparing her for life as a university student.

Tommy was born the following summer. Sheana had loved him from the moment she set eyes on the tiny sleeping bundle, and had almost changed her mind about leaving Creagbowie to start her degree in botany.

Angelina had been singing at a charity concert when the most cruel blow of all had befallen the family. Returning home at the end of the winter evening, with their young son asleep in the back of the car, the lives of Robert and his talented wife had been cut cruelly short. A drunken driver had hit their car head on, killing them instantly, leaving five-year-old Tommy badly injured.

Sheana had resigned from teaching as soon as she could be released from her contract. She had returned to Creagbowie to support Aunt Ellie in the care of her young half-brother, and to do her best to run Creagbowie Farm. It was Tommy's inheritance and their only means of support.

Eventually she hoped to resume her teaching career if she could find work nearer home, but she knew Aunt Ellie appreciated her help and company in the weeks and months following the accident. Although she was extremely fit for her fifty-seven years, the shock and anxiety had taken its toll.

Tommy's courage had been an example to them all. The doctors and nurses had taken him to their hearts and given him all the care and encouragement they could. Gradually his broken bones had healed and he was persevering with his exercises, but he had retained a paralysing fear of travelling in a car.

The doctors believed this was exacerbated by his inability to see more than a few feet while one eye remained covered following a delicate operation to repair the damage caused by the accident, but Aunt Ellie had great faith in the surgeon's skill.

*   *   *

As Sheana had predicted, Eleanor Lyon had seen Mike Bain's arrival and Sheana's look of consternation. Mike was a likeable young man and she quickly set another place for lunch. She felt Sheana was missing out on a social life since she had returned to Creagbowie and its responsibilities, so she had been sorry to learn Mike was already happily married.

Sheana had broken off her relationship with William Bennett, a fellow teacher when he objected to her returning home. They had parted in anger and Ellie suspected Sheana had found him wanting when her own need of

15

love and support had been greatest.

'So what bad news have you brought us, Mike?' she asked as he entered the kitchen.

'We can't hide anything from you can we, Aunt Ellie?' Sheana sighed and told her there had been a last-minute objection to their planning application.

'But who would want to object?' she asked in dismay.

'I havena heard who lodged the objection yet, Miss Lyon,' Mike admitted, 'but they went straight to the top. All objections have to be made public though to give the other side an opportunity to appeal. But . . .'

'But it will mean a delay,' Sheana finished for him. 'A delay we can't afford if we're to be up and running this summer. She spooned up the last of her soup, gathered the dishes together and carried them to the sink. At the door she turned to face Mike and Aunt Ellie, squaring her slim shoulders. 'Whoever it is they can't do this to us. We shall fight them. Do you know what grounds they are using for their objections, Mike?'

'My boss said something about "rights of way" and no proper access. Er . . . you are sure the boundaries marked on your plan are correct? They are the legal boundaries for Creagbowie?'

'Of course I'm sure. They're the boundaries we've always had. The deeds are with Dad's lawyers, but I could ask them to check if you

16

think we should?' She frowned. 'If it concerns the boundaries perhaps it is the people who have bought Fingaeli?'

'At least they could have come and discussed it with us. Mr Jamieson and his wife lived there for about thirty years. We never had a wrong word from them. Sheana's father always allowed them to use our farm track and walk across the bottom field when they wanted to take a short cut to the shore. When I was young it was a family called Dean who owned Fingaeli. They used the farm road, too,' Aunt Ellie said.

'Mmm . . .' Mike frowned thoughtfully. 'Sometimes when a path has been used over a long period it becomes a public right of way. I wonder . . . Anyway,' he shrugged, 'as soon as I hear anything definite I'll let you know. It may be that the new owners at Fingaeli assume they own the road down to the shore—I mean if your family always allowed the previous owners to use it.'

'Do you know who they are? The new owners of Fingaeli?' Aunt Ellie asked. 'Perhaps we should pay a neighbourly call? There's not the same divisions of class now as there were when I was young.'

'I heard it was a development company. I'll try and find out what their plans are,' Mike promised. 'I'll give you a ring tomorrow. Thanks for the lunch, Miss Lyon. The soup was delicious.'

*   *   *

Sheana was dismayed when she answered
Mike Bain's call the following afternoon.

'It is a company called A. & D. F.
Developments who have bought Fingaeli. The
personal assistant to the managing director has
already moved in there. Councillor Cobber is
being his most infuriating self, hinting that he
knows more about the company and their
plans than anyone else.

'He reckons they're going to develop
Fingaeli House and the grounds into some sort
of exclusive training centre for businessmen,
with individual apartments in the grounds.
Cobber reckons they'll bring a lot more work
for the locals than a caravan site and he's
already taking the credit!

'Just the sort of angle to attract the approval
of local councillors, and newspapers too. No
plans have been submitted through our office
yet though. Until they do we'll take Councillor
Cobber's posturing with a pinch of salt.'

'There isn't all that much land to build
apartments at Fingaeli House,' Sheana said,
'but their objection to our site, it will mean
delays whatever happens.'

'Yes, I'm afraid it will.' Mike heard the
anxiety in her voice and wished he could offer
a more comforting reply. 'I'll let you know
after the meeting. You can ask to be present,

or have a representative to listen to the objections so that you can appeal. The trouble is . . .' he hesitated, then hurried on, 'if the company is as wealthy and influential as Cobber is suggesting they might be pretty ruthless about getting their own way.'

'Oh no!' Sheana groaned despairingly. 'Anything like that would ruin us. Even building residential apartments will be detrimental. But Mike! I've just had a thought. The only way into Fingaeli grounds is through the big iron gates, just before you come to our road. There is a stile and a sort of kissing gate at the back of Fingaeli. The previous owners used it as a short cut on to our land to get down to the shore.

'You don't suppose this firm could be trying to claim it as a right of way so they could get a side entrance to Fingaeli, do you? It would ruin our proposals if they get permission to use our farm road, but it would ruin the character and charm of Fingaeli if they made a road through the front gardens. The grounds used to be beautiful.'

*　　　*　　　*

Ten days later Sheana was no further forward with her plans and she was growing increasingly frustrated. Her volunteer helper, Mr Kerr, offered to bring his grandson to help.

'But supposing we never get permission . . . ?'

'Dinna look saw worried, lassie. The locals will back ye up if these fancy folks frae Fingaeli try any tricks. Have ye seen the woman who has moved in there yet? A real snooty piece she is. She told Mistress Maloney at the post office if she couldna arrange for a relief worker she shouldna be taking a break tae eat her dinner!'

'Pay a relief worker? For the village post office?' Sheana laughed in disbelief.

' 'Tis true. Miss High an' Mighty said it was no way tae run a business and the folks around here need a good shake up. She's going to complain to the post office headquarters.'

'Oh surely not.'

'Och, not to worry. Ye ken Mistress Maloney when she gets her dander up.' His wrinkled face split into a wicked grin. 'She told her ladyship she could waggle her fancy behind all the way tae the town post office for all she cared.'

Sheana bit back a smile. Mistress Maloney had a heart of gold but she had the sharpest of tongues if anyone crossed her. The local people knew they were lucky to have retained the village post office with all the threats of closure, and it was mainly due to Mistress Maloney and her innovations.

'So? We'll go ahead with the boundary fencing then?' Mr Kerr prompted.

'Yes, why not!' Sheana tossed her head defiantly and resumed her daily treks with the old tractor down the track by the side of Fingaeli House first thing every morning, taking more fencing supplies.

*   *   *

'You will go ever so slow, won't you, Sheana,' Tommy pleaded anxiously, as he always did when she wheeled him out to the car for his visit to the hospital. She knew it took all the courage his young heart could muster just to get inside the vehicle.

'You know I shall be extra, extra careful when I have such a precious cargo, Tommy.' She smiled and bent to kiss his cheek, before she helped him into the passenger seat and strapped him in. She folded the wheelchair and stowed it in the boot. As usual Sheana eased the car into gear and moved slowly round the farm yard before driving on to the narrow public road. She had found this gave Tommy confidence and she could increase speed gradually as he became accustomed to moving forward.

Sheana saw the shining green and silver Mercedes through the rear view mirror. It was coming up fast behind them. For an awful moment she didn't think it would be able to stop. Moments later the car was revving and blasting the horn.

Sheana sensed Tommy cringing even further down in his seat, his small fist clenched. This was an exceptionally narrow country road with a series of twists and turns.

There was absolutely no question of overtaking, or of rushing around the bends at speed, even without a terrified child aboard. The driver behind would have to curb his impatience. Even vets and doctors did not speed on this kind of road.

Sheana didn't recognise the expensive car edging even nearer to her side wing. A prolonged blare of the horn rent the air. Tommy screamed and grabbed Sheana's arm. The car skidded violently. Sheana's knuckles were white as she clenched the wheel, struggling to keep the car out of the ditch. The noise was an assault on the strongest of ears and nerves.

'They're coming! They're coming!' Tommy shrilled. His eyes were screwed tightly shut. He was hanging on to Sheana's arm, petrified with fear. 'Don't let them take me away . . .' he sobbed pitifully.

'Hush, Tommy dear. Please, hush little one . . .' Sheana was trembling with anger and shock. One of her front wheels was almost into the ditch. An inch more and Tommy at least would have been catapulted at the windscreen. 'Hush . . . it's not an ambulance, my lamb, nor the fire engine . . .' She stroked the damp tendrils of hair back from his forehead. 'It's

22

just a very bad driver,' she muttered through gritted teeth.

'Is it the one who killed Mummy and Daddy?' He shuddered, staring into her face with his uncovered eye.

'No. He will never drive again.' There was an impatient knocking on the window. Gently she unclasped his fingers from her arm. She could feel him shaking and her anger rose. A woman in a smart green suit which almost matched her car was gesturing rudely. Sheana pressed the window button, her grey eyes sparking with anger.

'If you ever do a thing like that again I'll have you sued for dangerous driving!' she said through tight lips. The woman opened her mouth, it closed slowly like a stranded fish. Even under the make up Sheana saw her colour rise.

'Don't you dare speak to me like that! Do you know who I am?'

'I don't know, and I don't care. Drivers like you should never be allowed on the road . . .' Sheana felt Tommy's hand clutching her sleeve again. She could hear his soft whimper as he strove for control.

'Drivers like me! You are the stupid driver who is dawdling. And your spoiled brat shouldn't be allowed to hang on to you like that. You could . . .'

'You!' Sheana caught her breath and bit back the words she longed to utter. 'You

23

almost caused another nasty accident. This is not a road for speeding, or for overtaking, so mind how you drive in future or you might find yourself in jail too.'

Sheana glared at the well manicured nails holding on to the open window. 'Now, if you'll remove yourself. And your car . . .' She pressed the window button and wished she dared shut it faster. The woman snatched her hand away and almost stumbled backwards on her black patent heels. Her chest puffed out with indignation.

'You'll pay for this, you country bumpkin.' Charlene Dee-Smythe forgot to assume her lady of the manor act when her temper was roused.

She waited for the woman to reverse, which she did with a furious grinding of gears and hiccupping jerks. Sheana slipped the car into reverse and eased it away from the edge of the ditch, then straightened up. Only then did she realise she was trembling, or that her own brow was damp.

CHAPTER THREE

It was late afternoon before Charlene's persistence by-passed Miss Pringle's guardianship of Dean Fawcette. Even the most perfect personal assistant had to attend the needs of nature or make a cup of coffee, she reasoned. Miss Pringle's new assistant was a capable woman in her mid thirties, but she was not yet familiar with the 'who's who' of the Fawcette Company. She was certainly not proof against the wiles of a woman like Charlene.

On this occasion she decided to elevate her own position. Instead of giving her name she announced herself confidently as Mr Dean Fawcette's fiancée.

'Hello? Who is this?' Dean's voice was brisk. Charlene smiled to herself. She was aware of the barely disguised irritation.

'Hello darling. It's me, Charlene. I . . .'

'Charlene! For God's sake! You'll be spreading stupid rumours all over the office! Why didn't you give your name? No, don't answer!' He sighed impatiently. 'I'm due in a meeting in one minute flat. Couldn't . . .'

'But Dean dearest, I needed to speak to you.' She pouted full red lips at the telephone and made a kissing sound. There was no response. 'You did say this project was very important—more important than mere money—though I can't imagine why in this God forsaken part of the world.'

'Obviously I was right then, you don't like it up there,' Dean said dryly. 'I confess I was surprised when you insisted on dealing with such a small problem yourself.'

'The locals are uncivilised and they drive

25

like imbeciles. The officials conduct their business as though next year will do. As for the local councillor, he assures me he can use his influence to get the plans for the caravan site thrown out. He clicked his fat fingers to make it seem simple but in the next breath he hinted he would need some inducement . . .'

'You've never had any difficulty with men before . . .'

'I know a weasel when I meet one. This one will need more than charm. It will take money . . .'

'Money? And he's a councillor you say?' Charlene could picture Dean's frown. He rarely interfered with her work but she should have guessed he would never stoop to anything approaching bribery and corruption. She changed tack.

'I meant it will be expensive entertaining him. He likes the best . . .'

'Well put it on your expense account—as you usually do,' he added, well aware that Charlene's expenses covered anything from a cashmere stole to a bottle of expensive French perfume, or whatever she fancied from the hotel boutiques. Charlene looked at her new gold bracelet. It could scarcely be passed off as hotel expenses. Then there were several other personal accounts she needed to settle.

'I think I shall need some ready cash . . .'

'I can't see why there's a problem in the first place,' Dean said impatiently.

'You would if you met the rude young woman who owns the land for the caravan site, and her son is just a spoiled brat. He almost caused me to have a nasty accident this morning. My nerves are still shattered.'

'I see . . .' She could visualise his frown and allowed herself a smile of satisfaction. 'Charlene, I must go. I'll give the Scottish project some thought. Why don't you come back to London for the weekend. Recharge your batteries . . .'

'You think I should?' Her voice was eager.

'Yes, why not. Bye.' Charlene stared at the receiver in her hand. Dean had not given her time to tie him down to any definite arrangements. Still, he must be missing her. He would be pleased when she turned up at his flat. Pity the nearest airport involved a long drive to Glasgow or Edinburgh. Perhaps she should settle for the train. She could leave tomorrow morning.

*   *   *

Dean Fawcette felt an unexpected sense of freedom as he drove north on Friday evening. He had escaped from the office earlier than he had dared to hope, mainly due to Miss Pringle's efficient rearranging of his schedule. He would stop at one of the motorway restaurants for a break before continuing all the way to Fingaeli. No-one would be

27

expecting him so it didn't matter what time he arrived.

He patted the pocket in the side of his leather overnight bag on the passenger seat. There was a reassuring jangle of keys. He'd had a spare set made for his own use and only Miss Pringle knew where he was heading. She was entirely trustworthy. He had given her the number of his personal mobile phone with strict instructions not to give it to anyone else and to contact him only if there was an emergency.

Alice Pringle had nodded her smooth grey head and behind her spectacles her grey eyes twinkled like a conspirator.

'You work far too hard, Dean. A wee change will do you good. Your grandfather would never have expected A. & D. F. Developments to grow so big in such a short time.' A shadow of regret replaced the twinkle. 'It's a pity he didn't live to see what a success you've made of his little company. He would have been truly proud.'

'Yes.' Dean sighed. 'He gave me a strict training but he had already created the foundations for a sound business. You know that even better than I do. You were his right hand from the very beginning.'

Dean had the road almost to himself as he drove north over Shap. In the headlights the hills and sky merged but he sensed the wild vastness of the peaks and fells, the freedom of their isolation. His spirits rose exultantly. Miss Pringle was right, he did need a break. He had been far too overworked and tense of late. If he hadn't been so harassed he would never have allowed Charlene to go near Fingaeli.

The old house was a personal project, bought on a sentimental whim, though only Miss Pringle knew that. He had been surprised when her professional mask had been replaced by such enthusiastic encouragement.

She had always been proud of her own Scottish roots, even though she had spent most of her adult life in London. She had moved to the capital with his grandparents to be Andrew Fawcette's secretary and general factotum and she had quickly become irreplaceable.

Not for the first time Dean wished Charlene would take a leaf out of Alice Pringle's book. It was unfortunate that she had read the letter which Alice had put on his desk for his personal attention. It was from the planning authorities notifying him of the proposed development of a caravan site on property neighbouring Fingaeli.

Charlene had automatically assumed she would deal with it since she had become trouble shooter in chief whenever planning matters or disputes arose. He frowned. Charlene was quick to assume a lot of things . . .

He rubbed a hand across his eyes as the lights of Carlisle came into view. Another hour and he would reach his destination. A weekend away would help him get things into perspective and allow him to make the most important decision of his life.

Alice Pringle had listened intently as he explained the take-over bid, but she had kept her own council. She knew Dean was perfectly able to reach his own decision and her mind was preoccupied with a niggling worry concerning Derek Moxon, his chief engineer. Irrespective of Dean's decision about the company, as soon as he returned from his weekend break, she resolved to confide in him regarding Derek's predicament and her fears for his safety.

CHAPTER FOUR

Although it was well after midnight before Dean had settled himself in at Fingaeli, he was wide awake by six o'clock. A delicious feeling of anticipation crept over him and he stretched luxuriously. It was wonderful to have the day to himself, no plans, no timetable, no telephone.

He unzipped his sleeping bag. He need not have brought it. On his arrival a brief exploration of the various doors on the upstairs landing had shown him a large cupboard full of clean linen and five furnished bedrooms. He had selected the smallest one judging it to be above the wide front door which meant it would overlook the neglected gardens and the Solway Firth beyond.

He tried to recall the stories his mother had told him about the holidays she had spent with her uncle and aunt at Fingaeli, but he had been only seven years old when his parents were swept to their deaths and his memories were hazy.

Dawn was breaking and he moved to the large sash window to watch the myriad of colours creeping over the sky, sweeping away the shadows and showing him the long line of the Galloway Hills with the higher peak of Criffle, purple against the aquamarine, crimson and gold of sunrise.

His attention was caught by a woman running lightly over the sand towards the incoming tide. He saw sandals being kicked aside, a pair of jeans peeled from slim hips. His brown eyes widened.

Could it be the same girl? Why had he not thought of taking a dawn bathe? He shivered. The water would be freezing. It was early May. There had not been enough sun to warm the water yet.

He watched in fascination as the girl jumped and danced into the oncoming waves. He envied her joyous freedom.

He had not realised he was holding his breath until he saw her turn and swim back toward the place where she had entered the water and where her discarded clothes awaited her.

How gracefully she moved as she ran lightly over the sand, jumping over channels and rock pools carved into the machair by higher tides. Her hair still clung to her head but as she came nearer Dean was almost sure it was the girl he had met on his first visit.

He turned and headed for the bathroom. He pulled on a pair of jeans and a casual shirt and made his way to the kitchen.

The warmth of an enormous Aga cooker welcomed him and the sun shone on the mellow golden wood of the kitchen units. Suddenly he felt the weight of his responsibilities and experienced a pang of envy for the carefree girl who took her surroundings for granted.

He lifted the heavy lid of the cooker and felt the heat waft across his face. He filled the kettle and set it to boil before examining the contents of the cupboards. He found a frying pan to cook the bacon and eggs which Alice Pringle had thoughtfully bought for him during her lunch break.

'If they're not expecting you there'll be no one to cook your meals,' she had warned. Now as he dropped a couple of eggs in beside the sizzling bacon he was glad he had not sent word to Mrs McCracken. It felt good to have peace.

Dean was habitually tidy. He washed up and

left everything as neat and clean as he had found it. On impulse he explored the cupboards and found a good stock of tins. The fridge contained an assortment of salads, milk, cheese and eggs, as well as a packet of bacon and several links of fat sausages.

Mrs McCracken had probably stocked up expecting Charlene would be here over the weekend.

Then his expression sobered as he remembered the purpose of this visit was to solve the problem of the proposed caravan site.

CHAPTER FIVE

As he strolled along the winding roads Dean breathed in pleasurably, recognising the scent of early honeysuckle mingling with the dampness of the grassy banks.

His mother had been the only child of elderly parents and had spent some of her school holidays with her father's younger brother at Fingaeli. She had been an orphan by the time she was nineteen and had married his father before her twentieth birthday.

Alice Pringle had been her best friend and her bridesmaid as well as being roped in for her first job by his paternal grandfather. When his grandparents moved south to expand their small engineering business Alice had accompanied them as accounts clerk, typist cum general factotum.

Grandfather Fawcette had needed someone he could trust and Alice was the person. He had helped her find a pleasant ground floor flat near the offices. Later he had helped her to buy it, as well as the flat above. One of his grandfather's greatest assets had been his shrewd judgement.

He had known Alice was utterly trustworthy and had shown his appreciation of her diligence and loyalty at the end by leaving her a fifteen percent share in the company. Alice rarely mentioned her legacy. She made it plain she preferred the rest of the staff to remain in ignorance.

As Dean strode along he wondered how he would manage the ever increasing number of employees when Alice retired. He knew that day could not be far ahead. Once or twice recently she had mentioned selling her flats to buy a small cottage in her native Scotland.

He was barely aware that he had walked a good two miles or more until he approached some cottages and realised he was approaching the village. An old man working in his front garden looked up and eyed him curiously before greeting him and passing a comment on the weather in typical British fashion.

Dean smiled and returned the pleasantry,

but he was aware that in this small community a newcomer would stick out like a sore thumb. He admired the cottage gardens with their cascades of purple aubretia and yellow stonecrop, and here and there the flame of pieris or azaleas, the golden glow of a late forsythia, or was it a kerria? The names came back to him and he realised he had acquired his scanty knowledge of gardening from Alice Pringle and his grandmother.

He almost walked past the post office without realising it was part of one of the cottages. An old-fashioned bell clanged as he entered but the woman was already behind the counter. He bought a book of stamps he didn't need and then his glance alighted on a stand with local maps and he selected one of the area, bought a couple of apples and a bottle of spring water and set them on the counter.

'On holiday are ye?' the woman asked pleasantly enough, but with frank curiosity.

'Just having a short break. I'm enjoying your beautiful countryside.'

'Aye, tis a bonny part o' the country,' the woman beamed. 'If ye're looking for a place tae stay there's the new hotel along the coast, near the golf course. D'ye play golf?'

'Sometimes, but not on this visit.'

'Well then there's the wee hotel that used to be the old manse, just a mile or so the other way. Or maybe ye're camping? Ye'd find a spot at Creagbowie Farm. Miss Sheana has great plans to develop the site to take in caravans now she's home to look after the wee fellow. It will bring more trade for me and the other wee businesses. She's run into a problem though.'

'A problem . . . ?'

'Aye. Och, not frae any o' the locals. I think . . .' she lowered her voice and leaned towards him conspiratorially, 'I reckon it's yon haughty woman who is supposed to have bought Fingaeli House. A tongue like a razor blade she has.'

'I see. Maybe I shall come across the campsite while I'm walking. How much do I owe you?' His tone was firm, putting an end to the discussion. He had a sudden desire to remain incognito. Charlene had certainly not enamoured herself to the post-mistress and it sounded as though she had exaggerated her position regarding Fingaeli.

He felt uncomfortable at the thought of her causing unpleasantness amongst the local people, however much he disliked the idea of having a caravan site on his doorstep.

Dean strolled right through the village then turned off as Mrs Maloney had directed, heading back in the general direction of the Solway. He hoped he was making a circular tour. He settled himself on a grassy knoll and munched happily on one of the apples while he studied the map.

As far as he could tell the road would eventually bring him to the fields which must border Creagbowie Farm. They might even be part of the farm for all he knew.

He walked on at a brisk pace. The road took a sharp turn and he thought he had come to a dead end at a field gate, until he realised that the road took a sharp bend and continued on as a farm track. He was about to follow when he realised there was a tractor on the other side of the hedge.

Every few yards it stopped while the driver dropped something onto the ground. It had almost reached the gateway before he realised the driver was a girl. She stopped and he realised he was staring at the mermaid of the early morning.

'Have you lost your way?' she called with a merry smile. 'Are you looking for the village . . .?' She stopped, staring at him in amazement. Delicate colour rose in her cheeks. 'It's you again . . .' she said faintly.

'Yes,' he grinned at her. 'We meet again. I was taking a walk to blow away the cobwebs. The woman at the post office told me I would reach the shore if I followed this road, and I understand I can walk along it . . .'

'You can walk along the shore, but it's a fair way to the hotel from this end of the sands. It's a good thing the tide was in early this morning. At least you'll not get cut off.'

'I see . . .' Dean frowned. He couldn't explain why he didn't correct her assumption that he was staying at the hotel again.

'Of course you could always walk across these two fields.' She waved her arm sketchily at the grassland. 'It would cut off quite a chunk and save you a long stretch of sand.'

'Mmm . . .' He looked at her, wondering how he could detain her, get into conversation, and . . . Sheana took his hesitation for fear and she laughed, a happy, musical sound.

'The animals won't hurt you. We don't run the bull with these. They're only young stirks. The locals often take a short cut via Creagbowie.'

'You live here? At the farm?'

'Yes. This is our boundary. Our fields come as far as the road on this side and we're bounded by our own farm track and Fingaeli House on our eastern boundary.' Her eyes clouded and a slight frown creased her forehead as she mentioned Fingaeli, but then she seemed to cast it aside with a toss of her head, and a swathe of silky hair flew over her shoulder. She looked at him doubtfully. 'I could give you a lift on the back of the tractor if you like? You'd have to hang on tightly though. It can be a bit bumpy.'

'Now that sounds like a splendid idea,' Dean accepted swiftly, lest she should change her mind.

'Don't hold me responsible, if you fall off,' she cautioned.

'I won't, I promise.' He grinned. 'Anyway I've no intention of falling off.'

'All right. I just have to drop off these last few stobs. It will only take a few minutes.'

'Stobs?'

'Posts. Stakes. You know, for fencing. I'm setting them out ready for Jim Kerr. He's a retired estate worker, but he's lending me a hand. He likes to do things in his own time. It suits him if I set the stobs out ready.'

'I see. Drive on then and I'll put off the rest of the *stobs* if you tell me when.'

The last post had been unloaded and Sheana turned the tractor across the field and they bumped along. Dean thought his insides might be upside down, or inside out, by the time they drew to a halt in a small neat farmyard, surrounded on three sides by whitewashed buildings.

Before he jumped off he couldn't resist lifting a swathe of thick shining hair which hid one side of her face from him. His touch was gentle but it took Sheana by surprise and she turned to look up at him and found his face closer than she had realised. For a moment they stared at each other.

'You have beautiful hair,' Dean said. 'Soft as silk. You must have an excellent hairdresser to put the streaks in so naturally.' Sheana stared at him speechless. Then the round 'O' of her mouth turned from surprise to a warm chuckle.

'There's where I get my streaks,' she waved blithely towards the sky sun, 'and it's all free.'

She sobered and coiled her hair almost shyly. 'I usually pile it under a tammy when I'm working, but I went swimming again this morning and by the time I had shampooed it and eaten breakfast it was still damp.'

She sighed. 'Anyway it feels good to let it blow free sometimes. Aunt Ellie is always telling me I shall ruin it with the wind and the sun.' By now they had both descended from the tractor and were standing beside the huge wheel, reluctant to say goodbye.

As though she had heard her name, Eleanor Lyon came to the door of the house which made up the fourth side of the farmyard. It was white too, but flanked by tubs of bright spring flowers.

'Hello there,' Aunt Ellie called with a smile. She dangled a key on a short chain. 'Have you come to collect the key for the caravan?' she asked, coming towards them.

'No, Aunt Ellie. This is not Mr Madison. He is just out for a walk. On holiday this time presumably?'

'Just the weekend,' Dean nodded.

'I just gave him a lift across the fields to cut off the trek along the shore to the hotel.' Dean knew he ought to come clean and tell them he was staying at Fingaeli, but he found himself reluctant to reveal his identity and the reason for his visit, especially now he knew they were the neighbours intent on developing the caravan site. He bitterly regretted allowing

Charlene's involvement with Fingaeli.

'I'm sorry,' Aunt Ellie was smiling. 'I mistook you for one of our caravanners Mr er ...'

'Dean.' He smiled and held out his hand in a firm handshake.

'Pleased to meet you Mr Dean. Are you staying long?'

'Dean is my Christian name. Dean Alexander ...'

'Oh.' A fleeting shadow of disappointment clouded Ellie's blue eyes, but it was gone in an instant. 'Silly of me,' she said. 'Just for a moment I thought you might be a relative of the Deans who used to own Fingaeli when I was young. Never mind young man, I hope you enjoy your stay in the area. We're just about to have lunch. Would you care to join us?'

'But Aunt Ellie ...'

'I should be delighted,' Dean said quickly before Sheana could protest further. She eyed him uncertainly. Aunt Ellie would offer hospitality to everyone from the Queen herself to the scruffiest tramp.

'Come away in then, Dean,' Aunt Ellie smiled at them both. 'Sheana, will you show him where to find the cloakroom, while I warn Tommy and dish up the soup.'

'Warn Tommy . . .?' Dean looked at Sheana, his brown eyes widening. 'Am I likely to be greeted with a shotgun?'

'Not at all!' Sheana chuckled softly. He

41

thought she had a lovely laugh, warm and natural. It transformed her elfin face completely. 'Tommy . . .' Her grey eyes clouded. 'He—he's not very good with strangers. Aunt Ellie thinks it's good for him to meet people in his own surroundings though. She thinks it will help him get back his confidence . . .'

She frowned, reluctant to bore Dean with details of Tommy's ordeals and subsequent fears, yet anxious that he should not think Tommy a spoiled brat as that woman from Fingaeli had done.

'I see . . .' Dean was remembering Charlene had mentioned a spoiled brat of a boy. 'Tommy's parents . . . do they live here too?'

'No.' Sheana took a deep breath. 'His parents are dead.'

It was clear she had no intention of discussing her family with a stranger. He wished he could just have introduced himself truthfully as a new neighbour. His deceit irked him but it was too late now, and he really did want to get to know Sheana Lyon better before his true identity came between them.

CHAPTER SIX

The original house at Creagbowie was very old. Over the years each generation had made

42

adaptations and improvements, but the ceilings remained low. Dean ducked his head instinctively as he entered the kitchen. His first impression was one of brightness and welcome. A heavy beam bore evidence that two rooms must have been knocked into one.

Aunt Ellie busied herself at the cream-coloured range. There were cream painted units on either side and a large dresser with a display of china plates on one wall. The smell of her soup made Dean realise how hungry he was.

At the other end of the room was the dining table and beyond it, against the far wall, was a worn leather settee. Huddled amidst the squashy velvet cushions a small boy stared at him, one eye covered with a patch, the other dark with apprehension.

Small fingers tugged nervously at his black curly hair. Adjacent to the sofa, sunlight streamed through patio doors, highlighting the boy's smooth olive skin and thin face.

Dean was drawn towards the wide glass doors and the child, as though by an invisible thread. He was aware of Tommy shrinking back even further into the comforting cushions.

'What a beautiful view!' he said. It was true of course. The garden was bright with spring flowers and just outside the glass doors two tubs of bright yellow and purple pansies lifted their faces to the sunshine. He turned and met

Tommy's gaze steadily, but with a gentle smile. He squatted down in front of the settee, taking one of the restless little hands in both of his.

'You must be Tommy. What a lucky boy you are to have such a beautiful world right outside your window.' Dean meant it. Deep inside he felt a yearning to have such peace in his everyday life. 'There's a small mountain across the water, taller than the rest of the hills. I wonder if it has a name . . .'

He waited patiently, hoping for a response, though it was possible the child would not know the name. 'I like walking. Maybe one day I shall be able to go right to the top. I walk a lot now but I used to have a sore leg like you . . .' He tapped the frame which encased one of Tommy's legs.

Watching anxiously, poised to fly to her brother's rescue, Sheana held her breath. But Tommy raised his gaze to the face which was level with his own. There was a flicker of interest in his dark eye now.

'Honest injun?' he whispered.

'Honest injun,' Dean whispered back conspiratorially. 'But it's a secret. I don't usually tell people. Anyway it's better now.' He stood up and seated himself on the settee close to Tommy. 'But I'll show you how it was.' He hitched up one leg of his jeans. 'See there and there . . .? The scars are faint now because it's a long time ago . . .' Tommy leaned forward for a closer look.

'I see them!' he said triumphantly. 'Were you in a car crash too?'

'No.' Dean knew he had to tell the absolute truth to this child. He wondered what had possessed him to talk about himself. He frowned, aware that both Sheana and her aunt were listening intently. 'I was born with a funny leg. It wanted to go in the wrong direction. The doctors did a lot of operations to turn it round and make it normal. I wore a brace like yours. I—I hated it,' he admitted. 'But the doctors were right. It was worth the pain and the exercises. Now I can walk anywhere I want, and,' he gave Tommy a lopsided grin, 'both my feet go in the right direction.'

If only it was just Tommy's legs, Aunt Ellie, thought wistfully. He had been wonderfully brave about his physical injuries, and the doctors had promised he would be walking around in a few more months.

'Come to the table boys,' she said cheerfully. 'Sheana will you help Tommy up, please?'

'Will you let me help you, Tommy?' Dean asked. The little boy nodded, putting his arm on Dean's as he wriggled to the edge of the settee. Sheana and Ellie exchange astonished glances. Although Tommy remained silent for most of the meal he kept giving Dean a surreptitious glance as he sipped his soup. Dean met his eye once and smiled. Tommy smiled back shyly.

When Aunt Ellie moved to the cooker to bring a fruit pie for dessert Dean leaned towards Sheana.

'Would you come for a drive with me this evening and show me around your beautiful countryside? We could go out for a meal if you're free?'

Sheana's heart skipped a beat and her eyes brightened, then she remembered she had promised to babysit for Mike Bain and his wife, Jenny. She couldn't let them down at the last minute, especially when Mike had been so good at helping her over the planning application.

'I—I'm sorry, I have a prior engagement.'

Dean nodded. Of course she had. She was an attractive young woman and this was the weekend. She probably had a steady boyfriend.

It was only when Dean had gone that Sheana realised they had learned nothing about him. Where did he come from? What did he do for work? When was he returning home? Would he come back . . . ?

Dean spent the rest of the afternoon trying to restore order to two large rose beds, giving them a belated pruning and removing the weeds. He found a good-sized compost heap behind the old building which had probably been a pigsty at one time.

Determinedly he banished work and business from his mind and turned his thoughts to Creagbowie.

Eleanor Lyon had mentioned the plans for the caravan park briefly, but he had noticed Sheana's frown and her aunt had changed the subject. Surely they ought to be able to resolve their problems with a civilised discussion.

That was not the way Charlene handled things in the tough world of developments of course and he cursed himself for the umpteenth time for allowing her near Fingaeli. He didn't even know what she had done so far.

Tomorrow morning he would take a walk along the shore and see if he could find the exact location of the caravan site and maybe discover some alternative route. If only Charlene hadn't irritated the local people, but it was his own fault for not dealing with it himself. He had not yet told her Fingaeli was for his own personal use.

A large caravan site would surely spoil the amenities of Creagbowie, as well as Fingaeli? His thoughts returned to Sheana—the happy dancing girl. She looked as carefree and as graceful as a water sprite, revelling in her space and freedom. He couldn't get her out of his mind. A crowd of holiday makers would surely ruin her pleasure too. Money must be scarce for her to consider such a project.

Sunday dawned as bright and clear as the day before. Dean felt his spirits soar as he contemplated the day ahead. He watched until he saw Sheana enjoying her early morning swim again. He should have told her the truth.

47

Now he found he didn't want Sheana Lyon to know of his connection with Charlene and her brash approach to problems—at least not until he knew her well enough to explain.

Over breakfast he decided to spend another night at Fingaeli. He would phone Alice and ask her to transfer Charlene to the German project. There were enough problems there to satisfy her. The German directors would need all her ruthless ingenuity.

Having made up his mind he settled down to another cup of coffee and considered how he would explain his presence at Fingaeli to Sheana and her family. He didn't enjoy deceiving or being deceived. He glanced at his watch. It would be inconsiderate to telephone Alice so early on a Sunday morning.

His mind raced as he considered how he might help Sheana and her family maintain their independence without spoiling the peaceful surroundings. The problem was he didn't know the area well enough. He needed to know more about their plans, their boundaries, their needs . . . He was too preoccupied to enjoy a long walk and he returned to Fingaeli to telephone Alice Pringle.

The telephone was engaged for a long time and he guessed Alice was checking her small share portfolio and generally browsing on the internet, indulging in her favourite pastime.

'Ah, Dean!' she greeted him warmly when

he eventually got through. 'I'm afraid you're in hot water . . .' He could tell from the lilt in her voice that she did not consider the trouble serious.

'What have I forgotten?' he asked wryly.

'You forgot to tell Miss Smith what your plans were for the weekend of course. I had great difficulty fending her off all day yesterday.'

'But it was Saturday . . .'

'I know. Unfortunately Miss Smith persuaded the duty secretary to give her my number. She had already tried to get you several times. She had been round to your flat on Friday evening and waited quite some time I believe.'

'Blast! Alice, I'm so sorry if Charlene has pestered you.'

'I simply told her I could not get you on your usual number either, which was perfectly true of course.' He could hear the smile in her voice.

'Of course,' he echoed, grinning at the telephone. 'Well, I've decided to stay here another night. I'll drive back tomorrow.' He gave her the instructions about the German project and asked her to pass them on to Charlene first thing on Monday.

It was very late in the afternoon when Dean gazed with satisfaction at the large heap of branches he had cleared from the shrubbery. There was still a great deal to do, but with luck he would return next weekend, then he could clear more rubbish and make a bonfire.

As he worked, his thoughts had been on Creagbowie and its occupants. He had made up his mind to call at the little farm in the morning before he set off back to London. He would tell them who he was. Somehow he would convince them that he wanted to be neighbourly, even though he could not agree to having caravans shunting up and down the track beside the Fingaeli boundary.

Neighbourly? Was that all he wanted? He thought of Sheana dancing amidst the waves. He wanted to know more, much more about her. He was certain he could find a solution. If only Sheana would give him all the facts and discuss her plans . . . The telephone was ringing as he entered the hall.

'Alice? Is something wrong?'

'I've tried to get you all afternoon.'

'Sorry. I've been working in the garden and I left my mobile in the kitchen. There's no answer phone here. I shall need to get one . . .'

'Miss Smith telephoned me.'

'Charlene? On a Sunday?'

'Yes. She was on her mobile. She sounded very put out.'

'Mmm. Did you tell her to prepare for the trip to Germany?'

'No, I didn't get a chance. She said she had been round to your flat again and it was quite ridiculous that she couldn't contact you. She

50

sounded very irritable. She was speaking from the train.'

'The train? Which train?'

'She will be half way to Carlisle by now, I imagine. She sounded as though she was breathing fire. She's determined to finish off the business with the caravan site once and for all and without delay.'

Dean breathed an expletive which was not quite inaudible. Miss Pringle chuckled. 'I fear you may have some explaining to do. She says she will deal with you in person when she returns. She will not have to wait so long when she finds you at Fingaeli.'

CHAPTER SEVEN

Dean's first thought was to pack up and leave Fingaeli immediately, but then his jaw set stubbornly. 'This is my house, my future home,' he muttered and made up his mind that neither Charlene, nor anyone else, would drive him away.

He cooked a steak he had taken out of the freezer that morning, and explored the contents of the vegetable drawer in the refrigerator. He rarely cooked, but as he prepared a substantial salad to go with the steak he realised he was enjoying himself.

Replete once more, he spared a thought for

Charlene and wondered what time she would arrive. The trains were often delayed on Sundays due to repairs on the track. Tomorrow morning would be time enough to impress upon her the importance of avoiding unpleasantness with the local people. He grinned to himself as he imagined her surprise at finding him at Fingaeli.

Charlene was astonished. She was also furious when she realised he had spent the whole weekend at Fingaeli.

'I've had a hell of a journey! I needn't have gone to London. Why didn't you let me know you were coming up?' Her green eyes narrowed. 'Or was it that Pringle witch? I can just imagine her deliberately misleading me . . .'

'My visit to Fingaeli was a spur of the moment decision and nothing to do with Miss Pringle,' Dean said firmly. 'Now sit down and have a glass of wine to relax you. I'll make you a light meal on a tray in front of the fire.'

'Fire?'

'Yes. I put a match to it earlier when the rain came on. Mrs McCracken had left it set. I'm delighted with the way she keeps things clean and tidy and well stocked. I've enjoyed my weekend of peace and quiet.'

'You've enjoyed!' Charlene's eyes glittered angrily. 'Well that's more than I can say for mine. Why did you come? I can easily deal with the stupid neighbours and their gypsy camp.'

'I don't think you need trouble your head over the caravan site, Charlene.' Dean's tone was cool and she knew by the way his dark brows had gathered into a frown that he did not care for her choice of words.

'But . . .'

'We'll discuss it in the morning. I intend to call at Creagbowie and try to reach a compromise. I'll bring you up to date before I leave. Now, you go and freshen up while I prepare a tray.'

'Well, don't I even get a welcoming kiss after my weary travels . . .?' She pouted and held up her mouth to his. Dean hesitated for a brief second then bent and kissed her cheek.

'Now go and get ready for your meal. You'll feel refreshed when you've eaten. You starve yourself half to death for that figure of yours.'

Charlene frowned as she made her way up the wide staircase. Was there a trace of criticism in Dean's tone? She was sure he liked his women smart and sophisticated. She had seen him around at business and social functions long before she persuaded an ex-colleague to introduce them.

It had not taken long after that before she managed to wheedle herself into her present job with A. & D. F. Developments. She was good at trouble shooting, and she knew it. She was sure she would have made faster progress in her relationship with Dean if it was not for the Pringle woman.

This was an opportunity not to be missed though. She had Dean all to herself and she intended to make the most of it. Instead of freshening up she ran a hot bath and poured in a generous measure of her favourite bath essence. As she soaked herself her irritation vanished.

She decided to put on her blue silk nightdress, but she could not face Dean without her make up. It took longer than she had intended before she descended the stairs and Dean had obviously been dozing in front of the open log fire, her tray on a small table on one side of the hearth.

He stretched and yawned.

'You've been a long time. I'll make some fresh coffee. I thought you'd decided to go to bed. I was just thinking of going up myself...'

'Oh Dean, darling! You can't possibly go to bed yet...' She performed a pirouette in front of him, allowing her robe to float around her slim hips. There was no doubt what she had in mind. Dean sighed inwardly.

If he was honest there had been times when he might have taken what was offered without a second thought, but something held him back now. He realised he should have considered this aspect of being alone at Fingaeli when Charlene returned.

'I have a busy day ahead tomorrow and I'm tired. I'll bring the coffee.' Dean frowned as he made his way across the hall to the kitchen. Charlene was an attractive woman. She was clever too and her conversation could sparkle wittily when she set her mind to entertain, but there was nothing subtle about her.

As he waited for the kettle to boil his thoughts turned to the girl who had driven him across a bumpy field on an old tractor, the girl who had danced like a water nymph along the shore . . . The kettle boiled. He made the coffee and carried it into the room. Charlene had moved the tray and was now languishing on the settee which he had occupied earlier. She patted it invitingly but he poured her coffee and stood up straight, feigning another yawn.

'I think I'll turn in now. I've had a busy day clearing part of the shrubbery . . .'

'You've done what? You mean you've been working like a common labourer? For heaven's sake, Dean! I'll find someone to do all that if it's what you want.'

'No! I mean I don't want anyone else to clear it. There's some fine shrubs in there. I enjoyed the work. It's very satisfying, but I've discovered muscles I didn't know I possessed.'

'Ah, now I understand. You need a massage.'

'We'll discuss my plans for Fingaeli over breakfast, but right now I'll go and jump into my sleeping bag.' He smiled kindly to take away the sting of his refusal. Charlene stared up at him in disbelief.

'Sleeping bag? B—but won't you be sleeping in the master bedroom? It's the only one with a bathroom,' she added with a note of contempt for the old Scottish house.

'I chose the room I thought would have a good view.'

'You'd be disappointed then!' Charlene retorted bitterly. 'There's nothing worth looking at.'

'On the contrary. The view from my window is delightful, quite delightful.' Dean's firm, often stern, mouth curved upwards as he thought of the Solway Firth and the lithe figure of Sheana Lyon skipping over the sand to plunge into its chilly waves. 'Good night, Charlene. I'll see you in the morning. I have it in mind to give you a job more to your liking . . .'

'Not the German development?' Charlene's green eyes widened expectantly. Dean responded with an enigmatic smile and she knew she had guessed correctly. She smiled like a cat with a dish of cream and patted the settee again, certain he must join her now.

'We'll discuss it in the morning.' Quietly but firmly Dean closed the door behind him.

*   *   *

Dean slept deeply after his unaccustomed gardening and it took him a few moments to

56

realise that the constant ringing was his mobile phone on the dressing table. He fumbled for the bedside lamp and struggled out of his sleeping bag. As he grabbed the phone he glanced automatically at his watch. It was not quite four-thirty in the morning. What . . .

'Dean? Alice Pringle here. There's been a— a road accident on the way to the Dutch site.'

'Accident?' Alice never wasted words when something was important, but neither did she panic easily. Dean could almost feel the tension in her now.

'How do you know?'

'A message came through to the office. George is on night watch. He phoned me as soon as he got it. One of our men killed, he said. That's all the details we have so far.'

'One man killed! Check the flights for me please, Alice? I must get there and see for myself.'

'Yes, I thought you would. I'll check Newcastle, Edinburgh and Glasgow shall I?'

'Please, and failing anything there try Manchester.'

'Right. I'll phone back as soon as I can get you a flight. You be sure and have something to eat.'

Dear Alice, Dean thought. No wonder my grandfather had found her such a treasure. He could rely on her implicitly. What would she do if he sold the company? She had only a few years to retirement.

Hastily he hurried to the bathroom, taking his phone with him. He had a quick shower and pulled on some clean clothes, cursing silently because he had brought only casual gear for the weekend, and nothing but his personal mobile for contacts—or had he?

He remembered Alice had slipped his smaller briefcase into the boot of the car just before he left. She believed in being prepared for any eventuality, but even Alice would never have expected anything like this.

He frowned, wondering what could have gone wrong. Derek Moxon always drove the small lorry carrying the explosives. He was a good man and completely reliable. No doubt there would be all manner of precautions surrounding the lorry on account of explosives but Derek would deal with the press all right.

He found himself muttering a silent prayer that no-one else had been hurt. One man dead was one man too many. He felt impotent being so far away. Dean always took his responsibilities seriously, but this sort of thing didn't happen in his company.

It was only when he was reversing the car out of the Fingaeli stable block that he remembered Charlene. He had no time to spare now. He would ask Alice to pass on his instructions about the German project when he reached the airport. His mind returned to the accident. Almost at the site Alice had said.

She sounded distraught. Dean was too

preoccupied to notice Sheana's slight figure walking down the track to bring the remaining cows in for milking.

CHAPTER EIGHT

Alice telephoned again while he was driving to the airport. 'Dean? I'm at the office now.' Her voice was grave and Dean tensed. 'The man who was killed . . . It—it was Mr Moxon . . .'

'Moxon! Moxon's dead?' Dean checked his mirrors and drew to a halt on a clear stretch of road. 'I can't believe it, Alice. He always drives carefully. He's our best engineer. He has a young family . . .' His own voice was gruff.

'I—I so hoped it was not Derek.' Alice's voice shook. 'I thought you'd want to know.' The news grieved her sorely. Could she, should she, have prevented Derek Moxon from going on the Dutch project?

She shook her head, trying to clear it, but her mind had gone round and round ever since the identity of the dead man was confirmed. He had confided in her less than two weeks ago. But he had sworn her to secrecy, forbidding her to tell anyone, least of all Dean, his chief, a man whose respect he valued beyond all others.

'He's not married,' he had declared. 'How could he ever understand how it feels to be torn between a job he loves, but which means being away from home, and a wife whose moods swing from jealously possessive to cold indifference?

'Maybe I'm to blame, but Julie knew how much I enjoyed my work. She knew that's how I earned such a good salary. She didn't turn her nose up at the money every month! I can barely take it in, Miss Pringle. I've thought of nothing else since I realised . . .'

'Are you saying you want to give up your job, Derek? I could have a word with Mr Fawcette. He wouldn't want to lose you. I'm sure he would find you work so that you would be at home . . .'

'No! No, please don't mention my problems to him—at least not yet. Whatever I do it can never make any difference now,' he added bitterly.

Dean knew Alice well enough to realise she was deeply upset, even over the phone. Derek Moxon's father had been with his grandfather since the company began and she had known Derek most of his life.

Derek Moxon dead! He took a deep breath. He must put emotion aside. He must get to the airport. He needed to be at the site.

*   *   *

Charlene had set her alarm to waken earlier than her usual time. She had a quick shower

60

and made up her face before tripping expectantly along to Dean's room. There was no sign of him, or anything to show he had been there.

She ran downstairs, but he was not there either. Eventually she threw aside her silk robe and dressed with her usual care, seething with angry frustration. What was Dean playing at? He had promised to discuss the job in Germany and there was still this stupid business of the caravan site.

Tired of waiting, she opened the back door and crossed to the stable block, part of which had been converted into a double garage and a workshop. Dean's car had gone. She turned and saw Mrs McCracken coming up the drive, eyeing the improvement to the shrubbery.

'Somebody's been working,' she remarked. 'If ye'd told me ye wanted a man to help with the garden I would have told McCracken himsel'.'

'You didn't know Dean . . . Mr Fawcette, was here?' She went into the house with a disgruntled Mrs McCracken following her.

'How was I to know! You told me you were going away.' Her tone was accusing. 'You never said himself would be coming. I would have come in, Sabbath day or no',' she said, aggrieved to have missed the new master of Fingaeli.

Charlene was satisfied. Dean had not informed anyone of his intention to visit

Fingaeli. She faced Mrs McCracken, her scarlet lips forming a brief smile.

'We didn't want to be disturbed . . .'

'But I hadna even prepared a room for him . . .'

'My dear Mrs McCracken, my room was adequate.'

'I see.' Mrs McCracken's tone was stiff, as was her back. She marched through to the kitchen, muttering, 'Well I expect he'll be wanting a good cooked breakfast.'

'He's gone. You know how it is. He wouldn't want to give the locals a bad impression.'

'Wouldn't he though?' Mrs McCracken's brow quirked ironically. 'But you dinna mind spilling the beans, eh?'

Charlene scowled. The woman's contempt was clear.

'Mr Fawcette is more than my employer,' she was stung to say. Her eyes narrowed. 'You can bring my breakfast tray to my study. I have a lot of work to get through this morning. The sooner I put an end to that miserable caravan site the better.'

'An end to . . . ? Ye canna mean Creagbowie? The farm needs the caravan site, what with all the changes in farming . . . The family have had a terrible time. Ye canna . . .'

'Don't tell me what I can or cannot do! Remember your place! A glass of tomato juice and one slice of wholemeal toast. And remember I only drink Earl Grey.'

Mary McCracken muttered a derogatory remark which was barely beneath her breath. She turned towards the kitchen, her mouth set. If this Smith woman was going to be mistress of Fingaeli she would not be staying.

*   *   *

Sheana was astonished when she heard the car engine in the grounds of Fingaeli. She paused to peer through the boundary hedge which bordered the lane. Someone had been tidying and pruning the shrubbery . . . but it was the sight of a sleek red car reversing out of the old stable block which drew her attention.

The hood of the car had been down, but it was closing slowly over the single occupant. Sheana stared in surprise, recognising him immediately. Why had he pretended he was staying at the hotel if he was a guest at Fingaeli? She could not mistake the man who had accepted a lift across the fields on her old tractor. The man who had shared their lunch and charmed Aunt Ellie with his excellent manners, the gentle way he had talked to Tommy. The man who had lifted her hair, his strong fingers delicately brushing the nape of her neck.

She trembled at the memory of his fleeting touch. It had awakened a yearning in her, a longing for someone to love her, and to love in return, a man she could trust and respect, who had strength and kindness in times of trouble. Her first impressions had been of just such a person. Had her intuition played her false then?

Charlene lost no time in getting on to Councillor Cobber. The smarmy little man assured her he had spoken to his influential colleagues. She could count on him to get the Creagbowie Caravan site proposal rejected.

'Twas not easy, you'll understand, Miss Smooth, it cost me . . .'

'Miss Smythe, Dee-Smythe,' Charlene interrupted impatiently. 'You needn't worry about the cost of bribing your colleagues I . . .'

'I didn't say I bribed anyone!' Mr Cobber denied hastily, 'just a meal or two to talk things over you understand, and a few drinks . . . The cost adds up though . . .'

'Of course, of course. We shall repay you generously.'

'The prospect of jobs for the area when the Fingaeli development gets under way had a big influence,' he assured her smugly. 'What sort of development did you say it will be?'

'The exact nature of the development will depend on the parent company. I'm sure you've heard of A. & D. F. Developments even in this neck of the woods,' Charlene said brusquely. 'I can assure you . . .'

'A. & D. F. Developments?' Cobber echoed. He had never heard of them until an hour ago on the morning news! He was not about to admit that though. 'They're the demolition and development company are they not? There's been an accident near one of their sites in Holland. At least one man killed. I hope there will not be any trouble of that sort in this area?'

'A—an accident? With the explosives? No! I—I mean of course there will be no problems like that here.'

'Then perhaps we should meet for dinner. Say seven this evening. You can tell me all about your company, Miss Smoo . . . er Smythe.'

Charlene sighed audibly, but she knew she had to humour the man if she wanted him to use his influence.

'Very well, but I do have a busy schedule. How soon shall we know for sure that the plans for the caravan site have been scrapped?'

'The meeting is this week. Of course the Lyon family may appeal. That would take another month at least. I know they had expected to be up and running within the next few weeks. In fact they have already begun preliminary work,' he added slowly, feeling a pang of compunction. 'A month's delay will be a big blow to them . . .'

'I'm expecting your committee to make it a permanent refusal of planning permission— not just a month's delay!' Charlene said sharply. She sensed his wavering. 'We'll discuss it over dinner this evening, Mr Cobber. I may divulge a little of the plans for Fingaeli, though they are rather confidential at this stage,' she said conspiratorially.

'Yes, yes of course. I understand how big business works,' Cobber said pompously. 'Though we don't want any accidents here . . .'

'Don't you worry about that,' Charlene soothed and put the receiver down.

She hurried back to the office and dialled Dean's mobile. There was no reply. Surely he should have told her if there was a crisis. Sullenly she punched in the buttons for the London office. She hated having to ask the Pringle woman for information.

Alice Pringle was still upset. She seized the receiver, hoping the call might bring more news. Her tone was sharp with disappointment at the affected voice announcing, 'Miss Dee-Smythe here. What's going on at the Dutch site? You should have kept me informed.'

'We don't have any details yet. There's been a road accident on the approach to the site.' Tension made Alice's tone unusually abrupt. Charlene slammed the phone down before Alice could collect her thoughts sufficiently to pass on Dean's instructions to go straight to the German project.

*   *   *

It was the end of the week when Sheana got

the letter from the local council. She tore it open eagerly. Aunt Ellie and Jock the postman watched as her anticipation changed to dismay.

'They've turned us down. They've refused planning permission for the caravan site. Oh, Aunt Ellie, what are we going to do?' Her voice shook and Ellie knew it was only her supreme control which kept Sheana from bursting into tears.

'Let me see, dear.' Dejectedly Sheana handed her the letter. 'It does say we can appeal . . .' Ellie said doubtfully.

'But that will be another month. The season will have begun. We shall be too late for this year's trade.'

'Why?' Jock asked with concern. 'Why have they refused permission? Everybody in the village was looking forward to you starting and maybe opening the farm shop next year.'

'They d-don't give reasons,' Sheana's voice trembled. 'Mike seemed so sure there would be no problem, at least in the beginning.'

'A-ah, but that would be before new folk bought Fingaeli?' Jock nodded. 'Now there's a haughty piece o' goods if I ever saw one. Staying in the big hoose and acting as though she owns the whole village. Treats Mistress McCracken and my kind like dirt, she does.'

'I'm sure they must be at the bottom of this,' Aunt Ellie said robustly. 'None of the locals would object.'

'Fingaeli . . .' Sheana said slowly. 'You remember Dean Alexander, the man who had lunch with us and who was so nice to Tommy? I saw him last Monday morning—very early.'

'Well he was on holiday and staying in the district, dear.'

'Yes, but he was driving a smart red sports car out of one of the garages at Fingaeli. He must have been staying there, spying out the land . . .'

'He was staying at the hotel so I can't imagine why he would be in the garage at Fingaeli. Unless . . . ? He didn't actually say he was staying at the hotel, did he?'

'We assumed he was, but he didn't contradict us.'

'Well it doesn't matter anyway. If anyone is stirring trouble it's probably that woman who is staying at Fingaeli. Mary McCracken doesn't like her one bit, and neither does Mrs Maloney at the post office.'

'And that makes three o' us,' Jock nodded vigorously. 'Now I must be on my way. I'll spread the word. Maybe some o' the locals will get up a petition for the caravan site.' He climbed back into his van and gave Sheana a thumbs up.

'I thought the blonde woman was the most officious person I've ever met, but why would she object to our caravan site?' Sheana said.

'She may want to assert herself. Some people are like that.'

When Mike Bain called at Creagbowie he verified their suspicions that the objections had come from Fingaeli.

'Mr Cobber drummed up support from some of his cronies with hints of lots of jobs for the area from the company who have bought Fingaeli. He says a caravan site would hinder their development plans.'

'Development? Jobs? What do they plan to do?' Aunt Ellie voiced all of Sheana's fears.

'Cobber was vague. I've learned the firm goes in for demolition work. They prepare sites for new developers, but they don't usually operate in country areas.'

'I see,' Sheana said, indignation rising. 'So they don't care what they do to our lovely scenery, or the village, or to little businesses like ours! Is that what you're saying, Mike? Because if it is I'm going to fight them. I'm going to appeal for our right to have a caravan site on our own land. We'll show them they can't do as they please. We'll stop them using our lane too.'

'But Fingaeli people have always used our lane as a short cut to the shore,' Aunt Ellie said in troubled tones.

'Not in recent years they haven't,' Sheana said. 'Not since old Mrs Gillespie grew too frail to go out. If the new owners think they can use it for their developments, they can think again.' Sheana tossed back her shining hair and twin flags of pink accentuated her high cheek bones. Mike thought he'd never seen her look so beautiful.

'One of the objecting councillors said there'd been an accident on one of their sites abroad and there's rumour of a take-over as well.'

'I did hear something about an accident on one of the news bulletins,' Aunt Ellie said, frowning as she tried to recall the details. 'Quite recently . . . but I don't think it involved the demolition firm.'

'It was certainly connected. I called in at the post office on the way here,' Mike said. 'Mrs Maloney said the managing director had been staying at Fingaeli last weekend, but he had to rush away early on Monday morning to fly over there. He'd gone before Mistress McCracken got to work.'

'Last Monday morning!' Sheana echoed. 'That's when I saw a red sports car drawing out of Fingaeli stables, wasn't it Aunt Ellie?'

'I think so.' Aunt Ellie nodded. 'You thought it was the man who . . .'

'It was him!' Sheana exclaimed angrily. 'The cheating charmer! The way he made up to Tommy . . . Managing Director indeed! He— he's a traitor . . .'

'Sheana!' Aunt Ellie gasped. It took a lot to rouse her niece's anger in spite of the copper glow in her hair. But it was more than anger affecting Sheana.

'Don't you see, Aunt Ellie? Dean Alexander

70

must be the new owner of Fingaeli. Pretending to be all sweet and friendly!' Her grey eyes glittered.

'But he looked too young to be director of a big company,' Aunt Ellie protested weakly.

'Dean Alexander?' Mike frowned. 'The company is A. & D. F. Developments, but it's a Dean Fawcette who owns most of it. Cobber said the present managing director had inherited the business from his grandfather, Alexander Fawcette. Although they're based in London now, the family originated in Scotland. The Smith woman told Cobber that anyway.'

'Too much of a coincidence having two Deans,' Sheana muttered. Inside she felt deeply disappointed. She had felt drawn to the man from their very first meeting. And it had warmed her heart the way he had gained Tommy's confidence.

'We shall appeal. We'll fight the company, however rich and influential it is. We belong here. We have a right to make a living. We must preserve Tommy's inheritance.' Her small fists clenched.

CHAPTER NINE

When he arrived back in London, Dean sat in his office, facing Alice Pringle across the desk,

71

wondering how he could bring himself to answer her questions about Derek Moxon's death. None of them would ever know the truth now. One thing was for sure, he had no intention of letting the slightest rumour leak out to the press. He owed Moxon that at least. Alice was utterly trustworthy and perhaps she had a right to know. He rubbed a hand wearily over his eyes.

'You look dead on your feet, Dean,' Alice said, pushing a mug of black coffee across his desk.

'Yes,' he grimaced. 'I need a shower, a shave and a sleep. But there's some things I must do first.'

'Whatever you have to do, I think you will do it better if you have a couple of hours' sleep,' Alice Pringle said firmly. 'If you would rather stay at the office I shall see no-one disturbs you.'

'I expect you're right, Alice. You usually are. It's certainly not going to be easy facing Julie Moxon . . .'

'N-no . . . I wish I was always right,' she muttered half under her breath. 'If only . . .' Dean looked up at her.

'You look shattered yourself, Alice,' he frowned, staring at her over the rim of his coffee mug. 'If only . . . what?'

'It's such a dreadful thing to happen. Derek was such a good man, so quiet and reliable—a-and a wholly worthy man,' she said with unexpected vehemence. 'I—I . . . Oh Dean, I feel I'm to blame for his death . . .'

'Blame? You Alice? That's nonsense, you weren't even there.'

'No, but I knew he . . . he was troubled. I—I should have guessed his mind would be on other things . . . What a blessing he was driving his own car instead of the company truck. He didn't have any passengers, did he? No-one else was hurt?'

'No. Ted Irons was driving the truck with the explosives and the other members of the team. Derek had insisted on taking his own car for some reason . . .' He looked keenly at Alice. 'What did you mean about Derek Moxon having other things on his mind?'

'He came to see me. He swore me to secrecy before he would confide in me. He said he had to talk to someone or he'd go mad. He looked so desperate . . . Once I knew what was troubling him I pleaded with him to tell you, and to take some time away from work. He— he said that was the last thing he wanted, and you . . .' She broke off and bit her lip.

'Yes, what about me, Alice?'

'He respected you more than anyone else he knew, Dean.'

'As I respected him. He was the finest engineer we have—had. But . . . ?'

'He said you were so busy . . . and—and you'd never make the sort of mess he'd made of his life. He said you'd never been in love—

at least not so blindly that you'd rush into marriage the way he did . . . Oh Dean, I feel terrible about it all. I haven't been able to sleep . . . '

'Then that makes two of us, Alice,' Dean said gently, rubbing his eyes. 'Derek Moxon is dead now so I suggest you tell me everything, if only to clear your own thoughts. Maybe it will help me sort things out with that poor girl who is now a widow, not to mention three fatherless children. What a tragedy . . . '

'I—I . . . It was about his wife . . . He was so upset. He really loved Julie . . . He said she'd often made out she was jealous when he was working away. Then he discovered it had just been an act—to throw him off the scent. He discovered she was having an affair.'

'No! Surely he was mistaken?'

'He came back a day early from that job in France. He found them together. I think he would have forgiven her if it had just been once, but they had been drinking. The man boasted that he was the twins' father. Julie had known him a long time. She married Derek on the rebound after they'd quarrelled. She was already expecting the twins apparently. Remember how worried Derek was because they were early?'

'Yes, I remember that. But they were both a good weight for twins.'

'Because they were not as early as Derek had believed. But he really loved Julie. He had

74

no idea they were still seeing each other. The other man had been in his home . . . whenever he was working away from home. Poor Derek. He said he felt his world had blown up in his face.

'Even if he'd had any doubts, they proved he was not the boys' father. Finding them together again made him wonder whether the wee girl was his, and he adored her. I—I suggested he should take a break from work . . . He was so distraught, Dean.'

'Dear God!' Dean breathed. 'No wonder . . .' He bit his lip.

'Tell me everything Dean.' Alice said quietly, but her heart felt like stone. 'How d-did the accident happen?'

'Well that's the trouble . . . As far as we know there was no reason for it. Ted Irons was not far behind. They were on the approach into the site. On one side of the road there'd been a quarry. They were approaching a slight bend in the road but Derek's car went straight on, crashed through the rickety fence, straight into the water.'

'I should have insisted he was not fit to be working,' Alice said. 'I feel so responsible!'

'Derek wouldn't feel anything,' Dean said quietly, by way of comfort, 'And no-one else was involved. Please don't be upset, Alice.'

'Sleep now, Dean. I'll give you all the messages when you waken. I expected Miss Dee-Smythe to be back a week ago, but she's

75

still in Scotland.'

'She can't be. She must have gone straight to Germany . . .' He stifled a yawn. Quietly Alice moved to the door and closed it behind her. He would sleep soundly enough on the chaise for a couple of hours, and think more clearly for it.

Sheana fumed in frustration. Dare she continue without the planning approval, as Billy Frost, the joiner was urging her to do? Mike advised against it. He knew the way the planning department worked, even though it was not the planning officers who were responsible for turning down the application in this case.

'You think we have no hope of getting planning permission?' she asked anxiously. 'Surely it is only a temporary hold up? Why would a big firm possibly be bothered about us? I'm more worried now about their plans to develop Fingaeli. They may spoil the peace, ruin our business before we even start. We are so small in comparison . . .'

'Maybe they're going to develop a holiday complex themselves—you know a luxury hotel with all the latest leisure facilities . . .' He broke off.

'Have you heard that for sure? About building a leisure complex?'

'Only Cobber's hints. He expects to be well recompensed with use of the facilities in return for using his influence to further the Fingaeli project.' Sheana blinked at him in disbelief.

'I expect the gossips are exaggerating.' Mike shrugged.

As it happened Sheana was in the post office speaking with Mrs Maloney when Charlene Dee-Smythe entered. There was no love lost between the village post mistress and the haughty woman from London.

'Now here's the woman responsible for ruining the lives o' the guid honest folks o' Creagbowie,' she announced with a gleam in her eyes. Sheana turned around to see who had entered. Her eyes widened at the sight of the arrogant driver who had frightened Tommy with her blaring horn and tried to pass on an unsuitable road.

'I have not ruined any lives!' Charlene snapped angrily. 'I am simply trying to preserve the environment around here. I cannot allow a collection of battered old vans to spoil the amenities of Fingaeli House. Fortunately the local council are in total agreement.'

'Scarcely total agreement with a majority of one,' Sheana stated coolly. The green eyes narrowed.

'You were present?'

'No, but I do know that. You forget this is a country area Miss, er, Smith. We are a close community. Very little passes without comment. We stand by each other. I intend to appeal. You can tell your lord and master he

77

cannot dictate to the Lyons of Creagbowie.' Sheana lifted her small chin defiantly and looked the older woman in the eye.

'I do not have a lord and master. And my name is Smythe. Dee-Smythe.'

'Your name is insignificant,' Sheana said and saw the angry colour stain the carefully made-up face. She had not meant to be rude. 'It is the managing director who counts, and I intend to find out who he is and why he is intent on ruining a good honest enterprise.'

'That's right, lassie, you tell her ladyship straight,' Mrs Maloney butted in eagerly. Sheana frowned. She could have done without an audience or the post mistress's interference, however well intentioned. 'It's a dangerous company anyway. We dinna want any developments and accidents here,' Mrs Maloney persisted. 'It's been on the news again about that accident at a site in Holland.'

'My company was not at fault. We have an excellent record. And I can assure you that the man's family will be well compensated.'

Sheana gasped at the hardness in the woman's tone. 'You think money can make up for the loss of a husband and father?' She thought of her own beloved father, Tommy's too, and his mother. 'If that's the way your company operates we don't want you here, whatever riches you might promise.'

'I tell you we have an excellent record!' Charlene raised her voice involuntarily. This slip of a girl with her cool grey eyes was getting under her skin. She stared at Sheana's faded jeans and skimpy T-shirt, but even as her green eyes narrowed she felt a shaft of envy for the long-legged coltish figure with the lithe grace of a young panther. The sooner she dealt with her and her silly plans the better.

'My company will offer you compensation. Maybe even a couple of thousand pounds,' she said in a patronising tone.

'A couple of thousand pounds,' Sheana choked. 'We've spent more than that already on plans and fencing,' she said flatly. 'But supposing you offered fifty times that, I wouldn't be bought by your company, and you can tell your managing director that. What's more if he was half a man he would be here in person instead of sending one of his minions to do his dirty work!' Sheana knew her own temper was rising and she strove to control her hasty tongue.

'I am nobody's minion! Dean Fawcette is my . . .' she gave an affected smile, which reminded Sheana of a cat who had stolen the cream and was licking his lips. 'Dean and I have a personal relationship. I have complete authority to act in his best interests. You will get nothing if you choose to fight.'

'We do choose to fight—every step of the way.'

'You'll regret it!' Charlene almost snarled. She turned on her heel and flounced out of the post office.

'My! She nearly fell off her shoes there. Great stilts they are. Not right for country places.' Mrs Maloney's eyes glinted with excitement and Sheana regretted that she had witnessed the confrontation, and knew she would enjoy embellishing it.

'She didn't buy anything,' she said despondently. 'I'm sorry I distracted her.'

'Och, she'll be back when she collects hersel'. Anyway I can survive without trade frae the likes o' her, lassie. Dinna fret yourself.'

'Mmm, but it sounds as though they're here to stay at Fingaeli. People like that can have such an influence on a small community like ours.'

'They can that. Mistress McCracken has made up her mind she'll not be staying at Fingaeli House with the likes o' her there.'

'But . . . she's worked there as long as I can remember. The occupants of Fingaeli have always been liked and well respected . . .'

'Aye, they set an example.' She shook her grey head, 'It's a pity folks like that have bought the auld place. I dinna expect they'll stay long but they could cause plenty o' trouble and strife before they go.'

'Yes,' Sheana agreed glumly, 'That's what I'm afraid of. But we shall appeal,' she added, lifting her chin and straightening her back. 'After all Councillor Cobber was all for our

80

plans before he knew about Fingaeli. He thought the idea of adding a shop and a playground for the children was wonderful.'

'He's a right weasel that one. Runs wi' the hare and hunts wi' the hounds, he does. I expect the Fingaeli folk gave him a bigger bribe.'

Sheana looked at her sharply.

'Surely not! You think he would take a bribe . . . ?'

'It may be against the law and unethical and all that, but I hear things in here as would make your hair turn purple, lassie. But my mother always said if your ain conscience is clear that's all that matters.'

'If that was Mr Dean Fawcette we met at the weekend, he didn't seem the kind who would offer bribes,' she said slowly. 'But then I didn't think he was so deceitful either . . .' Sheana broke off and bit her lip. Mrs Maloney was an inveterate gossip and she loved to exaggerate things.

'Have ye met him then?' she asked eagerly.

'I'm not sure. We had a stranger at Creagbowie on Saturday. He said his name was Dean Alexander. He didn't mention staying at Fingaeli but . . .'

'Mrs McCracken reckons he's a distant relation o' Mr and Mrs Dean who used to own Fingaeli. His mother was their niece or something. The Deans would be there in your Aunt Ellie's day. His grandfather was

81

Alexander Fawcette so I suppose he could be Dean Alexander Fawcette.'

'Then why didn't he say so?' Sheana demanded. 'He obviously intended to deceive us until he had found out what he wanted to know. I'm sure it was him I saw driving away from Fingaeli and I know somebody must have been staying there over the weekend. The shrubbery and the rose beds have been tidied up.'

'I didna think a man with all that money would do such work himself,' Mrs Maloney said doubtfully. 'He didna even let Mary McCracken know he was coming either. Devious! That's what these toffs are. You watch 'em lassie.'

CHAPTER TEN

Dean's visit to Derek Moxon's widow had been even more difficult than he had anticipated. He couldn't rid himself of the feeling that Julie's show of grief was contrived, though he tried not to be influenced by the version of married life which Derek had given Alice.

It had been Dean's intention to get the best compensation possible for Derek's family. It had not occurred to him the newspapers would dig out any angle to make a story, but apparently the first rumours of a take-over bid had leaked out.

There would be those who didn't know the details of the accident, who would claim the company was opting out of its responsibilities to a young widow and her fatherless children, irrespective of the fact that Derek had not been in a company vehicle, nor had he started the job.

He frowned and bit his lip thoughtfully. Whatever he decided to do he knew he could count on Alice's support, but he had no wish to add to her worries. Already he was concerned by the effect Derek's death had had upon her.

Having resolved to do everything in his power to avoid publicity, he was dismayed when Julie Moxon had made it clear she intended to make the most of her situation to get as much money as possible. He suspected the generous settlement he had suggested had only made her think she would get even more if she went to court.

He knew the possibility of claims and court cases would never have occurred to Derek, especially since he had not actually been on site. He would know Julie and the children were well provided for. All the company's engineers were insured in case of accident or death.

Dean insisted on that. In Derek's case he also had an extremely good pension fund which would pass to Julie in due course. Dean shook his head. He had never known Julie well enough to suspect her of being fickle, or greedy for money.

Charlene came into his thoughts. He knew she hoped to become wife of the managing director, but was she really interested in him without his company? She was an attractive and capable woman. Many men would consider her an asset to a man in his position. But he didn't love her—not in the way he remembered his grandparents loving each other, sharing, caring selflessly, the tenderness, the gentle humour.

How would Charlene feel if she knew he was thinking of accepting a take-over bid? He sat up straight. Until now he had only toyed with the idea. A mental picture of a lithe young figure, dancing through the waves of the Solway Firth, flashed into his mind. He remembered her warm smile and clear gaze.

He thought of the low, white washed farmhouse with its sparkling windows and red geraniums, the comfortable figure of Ellie Lyon bustling around her kitchen producing appetising aromas of cooking food. He had a yearning to escape from the pressures of running his company and the bustle of life in London.

At thirty-five he was too young to retire, but he had already turned down lucrative offers for his advice as a consultant to major companies. He could pick and choose his work, and his time. He could enjoy the hard physical work of bringing the gardens at Fingaeli back to their former glory.

He frowned. How did he know the gardens had once been beautiful? But he did. He had only the faintest recollection of his parents, but he distinctly remembered his mother telling him of the holidays she had spent with her uncle and aunt at the huge house called Fingaeli and the adventures she had had exploring the garden and the attics and the cellars.

He tried hard to recapture the memory, but he was left only with a soft merry laugh and the lovely scent of lavender which always seemed to float around her. He had been seven years old when his parents were killed during a landslide which had destroyed half the African village they were visiting.

His father had been surveying the possibility of building a dam and piping water to surrounding communities. His mother had only decided to accompany him at the last minute.

When Alice entered his office he was sitting with his elbows on his desk, a pencil held between his two forefingers. He looked at her over the top of it. His words took her by surprise.

'Did you ever hear my mother speak of her childhood, Alice, and the holidays she spent with her aunt and uncle?'

'Oh yes. Often. She adored them. That's why she called you Dean of course. She loved their house too. I went with her once you know. We were still at school. I have only a vague recollection of Fingaeli now, but it did cross my mind that you had bought it for sentimental reasons rather than as a development project, as Miss Smythe seems to think?'

He smiled then. 'It was one of my rare moments of madness. As you know, I had only a brief Sunday visit there before I bought it lock stock and barrel, via the firm of solicitors my grandfather used to use for any Scottish business. It has nothing to do with the company. It's rather large for a man on his own though.'

Alice looked at him keenly but she remained silent. She would love to see Dean happily married with several children running around. She was sure he would be a good father, but she just didn't see Charlene as a homemaker, but neither did she see her letting him escape from her clutches.

'I've quite made up my mind to buy a wee house back home myself when I retire,' she said at last. 'And Dean . . . That time is drawing close. I thought I might take my holiday in Scotland and have a look around.'

'I see.' Dean looked at her thoughtfully. 'This business with Derek Moxon has really got you hasn't it, Alice?' His voice held concern. She had looked tired and strained ever since Derek's death. 'I suppose it's no good telling you yet again that it was not your fault. There was nothing you could have done.'

'I can't help feeling I should have persuaded him to take a break, to talk to someone . . .' She sighed heavily.

'I understand. I should have realised he was not happy too . . .'

'And then there's the claim for compensation. If Julie Moxon goes ahead it will be a nasty business.'

'Aah!' Dean understood this was adding to Alice's worries. 'I don't think it will come to that, so try not to think about it. If you clear my diary I'll make a point of seeing Julie Moxon again tomorrow.'

Dean found his second interview with Julie Moxon easier to handle, if only because she and her partner made him so angry, and destroyed any sympathy he had felt for her on his first visit.

He rang the doorbell several times but there was no reply. A man across the road was working in his garden.

'You'll need to go round the back,' he called. 'Probably still in bed.' Dean nodded his thanks and made his way round to the back of the detached house which had given Derek so much satisfaction when he bought it. Children's toys were strewn around the lawn which was already overgrown and littered with items of rubbish.

He knocked firmly, determined to sort this matter once and for all. It made him feel ill to see Derek's home so neglected already. An upstairs window opened and the flabby white torso of a man appeared.

'What d'yer think yer doin' disturbing us this early? Go away.'

'I have business to discuss with Mrs Moxon. My name is Fawcette from the A. & D. F. Development Company.'

'Who? Oh!' Dean saw the man's small eyes widen and then narrow sharply. He knew that look and was immediately on his guard. He heard the man call over his shoulder, then back to the window. 'She'll be down in a minute.'

Julie was barely recognisable as the attractive, well-dressed young woman Dean had met with Derek. She had pulled on a purple housecoat over her nightdress and her hair was straggling and unkempt, and without makeup her skin had a sallow greasy look. The man who followed her into the untidy kitchen was dressed only in a pair of shabby jeans.

'My business is with Mrs Moxon,' he said politely.

'Come through to the room,' she said.

'I'll come with yer. Her business is my business. I knows your sort. Well-dressed toffs. You'll be trying to get out uv payin' her what

88

she's due.'

'You want to discuss your husband in front of—of this . . . ?'

'This is Eddie. He—he's my—my friend.'

'Friend!' The man gave a great guffaw. 'That's rich eh! I'm the father o' her kids. That's who I am.'

'Is that so?' Dean said coolly. 'You're sure about that are you?'

' 'Course I'm sure! I . . .'

'Shut up, Eddie!' Julia snapped. She was brighter than he was and she recognised Dean's watchful manner.

'Where are the children?' Dean asked. 'Will they disturb us?'

'They're having a sleepover with their pals,' Julie said. 'Sit down, Mr Fawcette.' She was gathering herself together now, wishing she had taken time to dress and make up her face and brush her hair.

'I've been askin' around. You'll need to pay us at least a hundred grand if you want to keep us out of court,' Eddie butted in, his eyes gleaming greedily. 'Even if he hadn't got to the site he'd be driving a company lorry so you're responsible.'

Dean felt his anger and his contempt rising. Pay *Us*! No wonder Derek had been disgusted and disillusioned, so sick at heart. Suddenly he felt a traitor to Derek, offering money to a couple like these two with neither principles nor loyalty.

After some extremely unpleasant insinuations from Eddie, with Julie backing him up, though increasingly half-heartedly, Dean was provoked into telling them Derek had confided in a friend about the insufferable heartache of his home situation.

'My previous offer was made because I had the greatest respect for Derek. I did not know then of the unhappiness you two have caused him. Had you not been so greedy you would have accepted the settlement.

'You don't need me to tell you the consequences if Derek's misery becomes common knowledge, Mrs Moxon. The newspapers will rake up the dirt about you and your . . . er friend . . . There will be some ready to say he took his own life, especially since he had insisted on driving his own car that day.

'In my opinion, if anyone was responsible for his death it was not Derek, nor my company, but you two.' He held his hand up to silence Eddie's protest. 'He loved Julie, in spite of everything. He knew she would be well provided for with the insurance, and his pension in later life.'

'You're just trying to wriggle out of paying up! He'd no reason to . . .'

'No reason!' Dean stood up angrily. He was surprised to see the blustering Eddie shrink away. 'Everything he lived for, worked for, everyone he loved . . . You, yes you—ruined.'

'She was mine first . . .' Eddie muttered, but

he could not meet Dean's furious eyes. Dean turned to Julie, his mind made up. 'I shall make provision for the children's education, as I'm sure Derek would have done. A fund will be placed in trust. You!' he glared at Eddie, 'You will not get your hands on a penny. Now I'll bid you goodbye. You will hear from the company's solicitors in a few weeks.' He spoke curtly, keeping a tight rein on his temper as he strode to the door.

As he drove away he knew he would hear no more from them.

CHAPTER ELEVEN

Dean felt he had no sooner dealt with one problem than another arose. When he delegated Charlene to handle negotiations for a demolition project in Spain he was astonished when she insisted she must return to Scotland first, especially since he knew she enjoyed the warmer climates.

'Go back to Scotland? Why?' Dean's tone was sharp and Charlene flushed.

'I intend to make sure that weasel of a councillor doesn't renege on our deal. I'll make certain the witch doesn't get her gypsy camp.'

'What deal?' It felt like months instead of weeks since he enjoyed his weekend at

Fingaeli. He hadn't intended Charlene to undertake anything else up there, especially when he realised she aroused so much animosity. Even in the first instance he had only agreed to her making discreet enquiries regarding the planning application from Fingaeli's nearest neighbours. Her remit had been nothing more than that. He had also been curious to know how she would feel about living at Fingaeli.

As it happened he had discovered all he wanted to know about the Creagbowie plans himself, and he had also realised he wanted to become more closely acquainted with its occupants, and without delay.

He caught Charlene's look of sullen impatience.

'I left instructions for you to leave Fingaeli and deal with the German project. I've had more pressing matters on my mind, as you should be aware after the death of Derek Moxon.'

'Oh I sent Bill Crabb off to deal with the German problem,' she said airily, 'I don't like unfinished business. I wanted to make certain that chit of a girl and her caravans were stopped once and for all. Cobber, one of the councillors, promised to use his influence. Now he informs me the silly creature has put in an appeal. She's going to attend the planning meeting in person. He reckons the rest of the upright councillors are all for supporting her this time. I suspect he just wants a bigger bribe . . .'

'A what!' Dean jumped up, his brow darkening. 'You'd better sit there and tell me what you've been doing.' His tone was icy.

'Oh don't be so stuffy, Dean. Whatever your plans for that Scottish mausoleum we don't want a two-penny caravan site anywhere near.'

'I understand the plans for the Creagbowie development are quite tasteful, or at least so far as I had time to discover before I had to rush away to Holland.'

'Tasteful! How could any caravan site be tasteful!' Charlene scorned. 'Anyway you've never told me what sort of development we're contemplating in such a God-forsaken place?'

'It seems I was right about your reaction to living at Fingaeli,' Dean said dryly and sat down again behind his desk. 'As a matter of fact my initial plans have changed.' He gave one of those enigmatic looks which so infuriated Charlene. He knew she liked to think she was privy to all his plans, even to his thoughts, but only Alice knew the details of the takeover bid.

'There'll be no need for you to return to Scotland. Just fill me in on what, er, arrangements you made with this councillor?'

Charlene began, unsuspectingly, to tell him how skilfully she had handled the locals and how she had got the plans for the caravan site rejected at the eleventh hour with a promise of jobs for the area when the development was under way.

'Jobs? What jobs!'

'Well . . .' Charlene fixed him with her green eyed stare. 'You were like a clam about the development so I used my initiative. I have the silly little man on my side now.' Charlene saw Dean's dismay. She glared back at him defiantly.

'We never make promises we have no intention of keeping. You should know that by now. And neither do we trample local businesses underfoot.'

'Of course I know that! I told that stupid girl you would pay her a couple of thousand in compensation. The silly creature scoffed at it. I expect she's sticking out for as much as she can get, but you can leave her to me.'

Dean suddenly planted his elbows on his desk, buried his head in his hands and groaned aloud. Charlene was astonished.

'Are you ill?'

'Charlene, just go to Spain! I shall go to Fingaeli. I just hope I can sort out whatever problems you've created. You will not . . .'

'Problems I have created! I? I'll have you know . . .'

'I'm ordering you to leave Fingaeli to me.' Dean's voice was stern, and colder than Charlene liked to hear. She stared at him. 'I don't understand . . . ?'

'Just go to Spain! Deal with the business

there,' Dean snapped. 'And Charlene . . .'

'Yes?' She rose standing tall and haughty in front of her desk, her wine coloured suit and cream silk blouse as immaculate as always. There was no doubt she was a very attractive woman, but there was no spark of humanity . . . 'Well?' She demanded sharply, not enjoying his critical gaze.

'Remember this company has a reputation for fair play. There will be no bribes, no promises we cannot keep while I am in charge. We can do without that sort of business.'

Charlene flushed. It was hard being a woman in a man's world. She was building up a reputation as a tough negotiator. She didn't want Dean and his high principles holding her back. In her opinion there were some things he should accept without scrutinising her every move, even though they weren't married yet.

'Very well. Shall I see you before I go?' Her voice softened. 'We haven't had any time alone together since the Moxon fiasco.'

'I will see you when you return from Spain,' Dean said abruptly. 'I hope to have news for you by then . . .'

'Good news?' Charlene asked as eagerly as a child, her haughty demeanour vanishing. She had great plans for herself and Dean . . .

'I hope so.'

'Inscrutable as ever,' Charlene sighed, and bent to drop a kiss on his mouth. He turned and her glossy red lips settled on his cheek. He wiped it irritably. He disliked familiarity in the office.

CHAPTER TWELVE

Dean let himself into Fingaeli. The old house felt mellow and secure and a million miles away from the world he inhabited daily. His irritations melted away.

On the long journey north he mentally reviewed his situation. Plans for the future chased each other around his brain. During this visit he wanted to get to know the people who had taken care of Fingaeli for the previous owners. He had no intention of being an absentee landlord, but the house itself was too large for a single man.

The company had expanded rapidly in the last few years, far beyond their wildest expectations. The prosperity of it was the reason for the takeover bid, but Dean knew it would have to be an 'all or nothing' decision. He had no wish to be a cog in a company of directors who met around a boardroom table two or three times a year, collecting a fat salary, experiencing little of the challenges, knowing nothing of the problems of on-site operations.

He was a hands-on man. Projects, people, problems, personalities, these were where his own interests lay.

The small family company which had been A. & D. F. Developments had grown too large for him to give his personal attention to every contract now. He could delegate, he had reliable engineers, but he was no longer familiar with the details of each project, and more importantly he no longer knew his employees as individual men and women as his grandfather had done.

This was a point on which he and Charlene had disagreed several times. Now Derek Moxon was a painful reminder. Dean felt he should have been aware of the man's unhappiness, even if he could not have prevented the accident.

On this trip to Fingaeli he had brought some of his personal possessions. He knew now how efficiently Mrs McCracken ran the house. Tomorrow he would introduce himself and give her some idea of his own plans.

He has brought essential provisions and he enjoyed a simple meal at the well scrubbed kitchen table, feeling more relaxed than he had been since the day he rushed away from Fingaeli after his last brief visit. In spite of the early hour he made his way up the wide polished staircase. At the top it branched to the left and to the right. He looked over the carved oak balustrade on to the spacious hall below.

'Yes,' he murmured softly. 'This really feels

like home.' No wonder his mother had spoken of Fingaeli with such affection. Her childhood memories had been happy ones and it was these accounts which Dean recalled most clearly about his mother. He knew he had taken a gamble, but now he was convinced it had been a risk worth taking.

As he settled down to sleep in the wide bed in one of the rooms overlooking the shore he gave a sigh of contentment. Tomorrow he would visit Creagbowie. He would smooth away any minor misunderstandings.

Dean awoke early, feeling totally refreshed and full of enthusiasm for the day ahead. He was a little disappointed when he stood at the bedroom window and found the tide so far out, leaving behind a wide stretch of virgin sand. A solitary man walked along the shore, tossing a stick now and then for his playful spaniel. There would be no early morning swimmers today.

Showered and dressed in casual cords and a sweater, Dean cooked himself a good breakfast, something he rarely enjoyed when working. He was just washing the dishes when Mrs McCracken arrived. She eyed him warily, peering towards the hall door as though expecting someone else. Dean greeted her with charming informality.

'I'm glad tae meet ye tae, Mr Fawcette,' Mrs McCracken said gruffly. She peered towards the door again. 'You on yer own, then?'

'Why, yes . . . Were you expecting someone else?'

'Herself isn't here then?'

'Herself?' Dean was puzzled.

'Miss Smith—or whatever fancy name she uses.' Mrs McCracken sniffed. She knew it was no way to speak about the mistress of Fingaeli House, but she had made up her mind she would not be staying once they moved in.

'Ah, you mean Miss Dee-Smythe! She's not here this time. In fact I doubt if she will be coming to Scotland again. I do have another friend I would like to bring though . . .' He was thinking of Alice.

He thought she might enjoy revisiting Fingaeli. Maybe she could stay here while she was looking for a cottage to retire to. It would be good to have her living in the area. Near enough for him to keep a friendly eye on until she settled in, and later, when she grew older. After all she was the nearest he had to family now. 'I think you will like Alice Pringle, Mrs McCracken.'

The woman sniffed doubtfully.

'If I'd known ye were coming I'd have had things prepared for ye,' she said in aggrieved tones.

'I'm not a slave driver. I don't expect you to spend your weekends looking after me, especially when I come without warning—as I shall probably do quite frequently from now on. Last time I brought my sleeping bag and slept in the smallest bedroom, but I noticed there are ample stocks of bedding so I . . .' he frowned, wondering why Mrs McCracken was staring at him incredulously.

'It suited me. I was only staying a couple of nights and I had no idea the house was so well equipped,' he said shortly. 'I must commend you on keeping everything in such good order. This time I helped myself to sheets and blankets. I appreciate your honesty . . .'

'But of course I'm honest! I've worked at Fingaeli on and off since I left the school and . . .'

'Yes, and I shall be pleased if you will continue. Shall I show you the bedroom I've chosen? There are one or two items of furniture I would like rearranged if we can find a couple of good strong men . . .'

'Ye haven't chosen the main bedroom this time then? Miss Smith said ye preferred it . . .'

'Miss Dee-Smythe has her own priorities. I enjoy the view over the Solway Firth and the hills beyond. I might make a few alterations when I move in permanently. The small bedroom I used last time would make a suitable ensuite bathroom, but we shall see about that when I have lived here for a while.'

'Ye're not going to knock Fingaeli down then?' Mrs McCracken asked suspiciously.

'Knock it down? Of course not! I hope to make this my home. My base, a refuge if I take on other work . . .' He was speaking to himself more than the incredulous housekeeper.

'Ye're not making it into a leisure centre either?'

'Certainly not! Whatever gave you that idea?'

'Well there's a lot o' rumours . . . Councillor Cobber said . . . or was it Miss Smith . . . We thought . . .'

'I see . . .' Dean's eyes narrowed thoughtfully. 'I'd be grateful if you would put an end to the rumours, Mrs McCracken. Fingaeli will be my home.'

This time he knew his way to the village and from there down the road to the right which eventually bordered the far side of Creagbowie Farm. He'd had a germ of an idea in his head ever since the last time he walked that way, but then he had met Sheana Lyon and everything else had flown from his mind.

Today he would walk as far as the road would take him. If his sense of direction was correct he should end up back on the shore, or thereabouts, but he was not sure whether an incoming tide would prevent him walking along the sands to bring him in a full circle back to Fingaeli.

The tarred road gradually gave way to a short farm track leading to a field on either side. It was just wide enough for a tractor, and bordered by hedgerows. Here and there a gorse bush lit up the darker green of the hawthorn with a burst of pure gold.

As he walked his decision crystallised. He would accept the takeover bid. He would withhold his family's name. He would have no personal involvement. Alice must be the first to know of his decision.

The farm track ended with a gate leading into a long narrow field. A five bar gate was securely chained and Dean climbed on to the third spar, balanced precariously, and surveyed the surrounding countryside. As he had guessed he could just see the glitter of the Solway Firth beyond the field.

It was further than he had anticipated, but his supposition had been right in general. He checked there were no animals in the field before climbing over the gate and setting off towards the shore with a brisk, long legged stride.

Halfway across the field the tops of two caravans came into view. So he had been right, he was heading towards the caravan site. All he needed to do now was to convince Miss Lyon that his idea for an alternative entrance made sense.

As usual he felt a surge of anticipation as his mind grappled with the logistics, but this time the property was not his, or his company's. He would need Sheana's agreement and Dean was not used to consulting other people once he knew his plans were viable.

CHAPTER THIRTEEN

Dean had walked full circle, returning via the sands to Fingaeli House, but not without feeling a pang of disappointment. There was no sign of Sheana, or the elderly man who helped with fencing and odd jobs. Now he was ravenous. He frequently missed lunch altogether when he was in London. His appetite must be due to the long walk and fresh air.

Mrs McCracken watched warily as he strode straight to the cooker and lifted the lid of the soup pan, sniffing appreciatively.

'Mmm, homemade soup. It smells delicious. I'm sure Alice would approve. She enjoys good food too . . .'

'Not like Miss Smith then . . .' Mrs McCracken said stiffly.

'No, not at all.' Dean laughed. The two women couldn't be more different, he thought, and yet both were good at their work in their respective ways.

'Would ye like to eat in the dining room, or would it suit ye better in the morning room. I've put the table in front o' the window. Nice view out to the garden . . .'

'Oh don't trouble with that,' Dean exclaimed. 'I'll just wash my hands then we'll eat in here. You'll take your lunch with me? I'd like to hear about the local people and the area . . .'

'W-well . . . I-dinna ken . . . I-I . . .' Mrs McCracken stammered in confusion. Dean gave her his most charming smile.

'Please . . .?' he said. 'I've a lot to learn about things round here—even Fingaeli itself.'

Mrs McCracken did as he asked, but she was too much in awe, and still too wary regarding his relationship with the haughty Miss Smith, for her to regale him with too much information. Even so she did let him know that all the locals were in favour of the Creagbowie caravan park and that Sheana Lyon was greatly admired and respected.

'I'm sure she is,' Dean agreed, 'and I mean no harm to Creagbowie either.'

After lunch he crossed the narrow lane and made straight for the little farm. It was Aunt Ellie who answered his knock. He sensed her embarrassment at once.

'If you're still at lunch I can come back later,' he offered with his most charming smile.

'Och, it's not that. We're finished eating. It . . . I . . .' She bit her lip and her colour rose.

'If that's Mr Kerr, Aunt Ellie, tell him I'll be out in a minute?' Sheana called cheerfully, wondering why Aunt Ellie hadn't brought him in as usual.

'It-it's Mr Alexander, dear. I er . . .' but before Aunt Ellie could say another word Sheana was beside her, her grey eyes flashing

104

angrily, twin flags of indignant colour highlighting her cheek bones.

'Dean Alexander Fawcette,' Dean corrected before she could utter a word. 'I am staying at Fingaeli for the weekend and I'd appreciate an opportunity to discuss your proposals for the Creagbowie caravan site?' Dean wished he didn't sound so formal, but he knew he had to get his word in quickly.

'So you've decided to tell the truth this time.' Sheana's lip curled with contempt. 'We have nothing to discuss, Mr Fawcette.' She attempted to close the door, but Dean put out a hand to prevent her.

'Please . . . I have a suggestion to make—to your benefit as well as my own. I owe you an apology . . .'

'It's too late for that!' Sheana said bitterly. 'I have nothing I want to discuss with you. Goodbye.' This time Dean had no option but to allow her to close the door, short of exerting force and he could scarcely do that.

He turned away, frowning. If he couldn't even talk to her how could he possibly reason with her, make his suggestions, convince her he wanted to help . . . Disconsolately he retraced his steps back to Fingaeli. Mrs McCracken was just leaving. She smiled at him.

'I've left a salad and cold chicken in the fridge. There's fruit salad too and a carton of local ice cream in the freezer. I'll be back in the morning.'

Dean nodded absently. 'Thank you, Mrs McCracken. I wish Miss Lyon was as amenable as you are.'

'Sheana, ye mean? Ye've been to call on her?'

'I tried. What a temper!'

'A-ah we-el now, can ye blame the lassie? She's doing the best she can to make a living for the wee fellow and you and your fiancée have ruined all her plans. But she means to fight . . .'

'So I understand,' Dean said, 'but if only she would allow me to make a proposal. I'm sure we could come to an agreement which would be beneficial to both of us. She wouldn't even listen.'

'Ye'll hae tae be like King Robert The Bruce and keep on trying, Mr Fawcette, but I have to tell ye, we're all on Sheana's side if it comes to a showdown.'

'Well I can't say you didn't warn me, Mrs McCracken. I think I'll clear a bit more of the shrubbery. Some good physical toil might help clear my brain and give me some inspiration.'

'I'll leave ye to it then.'

It was only when she had gone that Dean realised she had mentioned his fiancée. Surely even Charlene wouldn't pass herself off as his fiancée—or would she . . .? This was a different situation to the usual development problems she tackled. He swore under his breath and wished for the umpteenth time he had never let her near Fingaeli.

CHAPTER FOURTEEN

Dean did his best to keep a look out for Sheana in the hope of waylaying her, but on Sunday evening he admitted defeat and prepared for his long journey to London the following morning with a sense of frustration.

He knew neither wealth nor charm were likely to get him anywhere as far as Miss Sheana Lyon was concerned and he cursed himself for deceiving her. He had little time for people who played games with the truth himself.

He rose early the following morning with a feeling of dissatisfaction, but when he looked out of the window and saw the wreaths of white mist curling in the hollows, the glimmer of water, way out across the Firth, and the outline of Criffel against the morning sky, he knew this was where he belonged.

His gaze moved nearer. There was a slim figure slowly shepherding some cows up from their field towards Creagbowie farmsteading.

'Sheana!' he breathed. Seconds later he was pulling on his old corduroys, and tugging at a shirt as he ran down the stairs. He barely had time to push his feet into a pair of trainers before he was yanking open the door and running to the bottom of Fingaeli garden to push his way through the hedge on to the track.

As he had guessed it brought him out just behind Sheana and her charges. She turned her head at the sound of hurrying footsteps. Swiftly she turned back to her animals and tried in vain to hurry them, but they always ambled at their usual snail's pace from field to shed and back again.

'Sheana! I have to speak to you. Please!' Dean couldn't remember the last time he had pleaded to speak to anyone, least of all a young woman, or even an old foe for that matter. But Sheana Lyon tossed her head and walked on. He caught up with her easily but even when he practically stepped in front of her she simply stepped around him as though he was a puddle in the road.

Dean's patience dwindled and he clasped her arm to pull her to a halt.

'At least listen to what I have to say. I have a suggestion to make. It could benefit both of us I believe.'

'You and your fiancée have caused enough trouble with your suggestions,' Sheana said coldly. 'You didn't even have the courage to do your own dirty work. You had to hide behind a woman . . .' Sheana didn't hide her contempt but she knew she dare not look into his face in case she met his penetrating eyes. He would never know how let down she had felt by his deceit.

'I don't have a fiancée and there was certainly no dirty work to be done. That's not the way I do business.'

'No?' Sheana drew herself up as tall as she could and glared at him. 'Then what would you call worming your way into people's homes and not telling us who you were, or why, and what about wheedling your way round Councillor Cobber—even bribing him, if the rumours are true.'

'I do not bribe anyone.' Dean's voice was curt now, his mouth set and angry. He felt at a disadvantage. He had a sneaking suspicion Charlene might have tried bribery. His grip on the soft flesh of her upper arm tightened, but he was unaware that he was hurting and Sheana would not wince. Instead she set her mouth stubbornly.

'How can we believe that, or anything else? You can't deny you lied about your own identity. Even where you were staying, so . . .'

'I did not lie about my identity.'

'You lied by omission. Anyway it doesn't matter to me if you're the King of Norway. The fact is you've ruined our plans to save Tommy's home. I hope you're satisfied.'

'No, I'm not satisfied with anything. That's what I want to talk to you about,' Dean said, his voice softening. 'I have a proposition to make. I just want to talk it through. To . . .'

'I don't want to listen,' Sheana insisted clenching her jaw. 'Now let me go. I've work to do.' She glared down at his fingers still clasping her arm. His grip slackened but he did not release her. He looked down into her resolute face.

'If you were younger I would put you over my knee and make you listen!' Dean said impatiently. 'As it is you're too old for that— and . . .' he grasped her other arm and pulled her against him, 'and too damned attractive.'

Before Sheana could even struggle he bent his head and kissed her long and hard. When at last he raised his head his eyes had softened. He dropped his hands to his sides. 'Now will you listen to what I have to say? Please?'

His voice was gentle and Sheana knew he had sensed her yielding, traitorous body. Her cheeks were burning but she summoned all her pride and what remained of her dignity.

'Never!' She tossed her head defiantly and stepped past him, hurrying after the cows which had almost reached the gate into the farmyard.

Dean watched her go, expelling a long frustrated breath. Of all the exasperating women . . . In that moment he knew why he was so eager to find a solution to the problem of the caravan site. It was true he did not want the vans trundling by the side of Fingaeli at all hours of the day, but more importantly he did not want a confrontation with Sheana Lyon.

What he wanted was to find a good solution to the Creagbowie problem and earn her approval. But there was more than that . . . Even when she annoyed him he had to admire her spirit. Life would never be dull or cloying with a wife like Sheana . . . A wife! His eyes widened. Whatever was he thinking about?

He turned on his heel and hurried back into the grounds of Fingaeli. But the feel of her small soft body against his own stayed in his memory.

Dean went straight to the office as soon as he got back to London. He felt tense and frustrated, without really understanding why. Instead of telling Alice about his decision to sell the company he found himself telling her all about Fingaeli again, and about his ideas for making a new road to reach the caravan site from the other side.

'That way it would preserve the privacy of both Fingaeli and Creagbowie farmhouse. Do you see?'

'It doesn't matter whether I see, or not,' Alice said dryly. 'It seems to me the decision will be up to Miss Sheana Lyon and the council planners. Anyway wouldn't it be rather expensive to make a completely new road.'

'Only the last part of the road would be new . . . But yes it would cost a tidy sum. And Sheana is so proud and independent. Even if I could get her to listen . . .'

111

'You mean if you could get her to agree to your proposal you would have to find a way of paying for it without upsetting her pride?'

'Exactly.'

'I imagine that could be done. After all most people have to pay compensation to gain amenities to their own property. I'm sure her solicitor would advise her that is a normal procedure if you made a formal offer to him.'

'If only I could get her to listen! To discuss it . . .' he muttered in frustration. Alice bit back a smile. She could tell the girl, Sheana Lyon, had really got under his skin. And about time too, she thought with satisfaction. He needed a girl with spirit, and passion.

'She must be quite a caring girl if she has given up her own job for the sake of her young brother?'

'Oh she is,' Dean agreed promptly, warmly. 'But she's so stubborn.'

'Am I to assume you've made up your mind to sell A. & D. F. Developments when you're making plans to live at Fingaeli, Dean?'

He spun round to stare at her. He had been staring moodily out of the window into the busy road below. 'Why yes. I'd forgotten we haven't discussed that yet. I'm so sorry, Alice. How would you feel about it?'

'It really doesn't affect me all that much. I'm ready to retire anytime. I'd like to enjoy whatever time remains to me you know.'

'Of course you would,' Dean agreed

affectionately.

'I thought I would sell my shares and the flats and look for a cottage in the country, with a garden of course.'

'Of course.' They beamed at each other in understanding.

'You know, Alice there's any amount of room to make two good sized flats out of the servant's quarters at Fingaeli. There's no use for them these days and there's a huge garden if you want one of your own. How about coming up with me at the weekend? Even if you don't fancy Fingaeli you could take the chance to look around. I'd really like to have you living near.'

'That's kind of you, Dean. You're so like your grandfather.'

'Yes . . . well . . .' Dean frowned. 'Do you think he would have disapproved of me selling his company, Alice?'

'No. I think he would have considered this a good time to let go, even though you are still so young. The company has an excellent reputation just now. But if it keeps on growing it's difficult to keep a finger on everything.'

'My feelings exactly,' Dean nodded. 'Right then, tomorrow we'll set up a meeting and see if we can reach an agreement.'

'Very well.' Alice stood up. She had an absurd notion to ruffle his dark hair as she used to do when he was a boy. She paused beside him. 'How would it do if I wrote to Miss

Ellie Lyon and explained that I had once stayed at Fingaeli, and that my employer has offered me accommodation there while I look around for a cottage. Perhaps if I could make contact with her it might be possible to mention your ideas for an alternative entrance. I'm sure she would pass them on to her niece . . .'

Dean looked up with new interest, his frown disappearing.

'It would be worth a try, Alice. You're the soul of tact. Of course I wouldn't be surprised if Sheana suspects I've sent you to do my "dirty work".' He grinned ruefully. 'But I've nothing to lose. There's one thing I'd like you to do without delay. Write to the council and tell them we've withdrawn our objections to the caravan park. I don't like to think of Sheana having to go to the appeal.'

'Mmm . . . Miss Smythe will not be too happy when she hears about that.' Alice's eyebrows were raised.

'Fingaeli has nothing to do with Charlene. Once she hears about the takeover she'll soon wheedle her way into the pocket of one of the main directors.'

CHAPTER FIFTEEN

The following weekend Alice accompanied Dean to Fingaeli. She had written to Eleanor Lyon and received a friendly reply and an invitation to afternoon tea on Monday afternoon.

Although it was clear Dean enjoyed being at Fingaeli and working in the grounds, Alice sensed his frustration at being unable to contact Sheana. She was certainly making a good job of keeping out of his way. He had taken several long walks but he hadn't caught a glimpse of her.

Sheana's cheeks burned whenever she thought of Dean Alexander Fawcette. She couldn't forget his kiss, or rather her own humiliating response. She had been kissed often enough before, but she had never felt so agitated, yet exhilarated, so aroused, so aware, yet so fearful of being swept away by her own emotions.

Her instinct told her he was a decent, upright character, and yet he had sent that awful woman to bulldoze Creagbowie into oblivion, all because he and his obnoxious fiancée wanted privacy at Fingaeli. He had denied that she was his fiancée, but he had deceived them all over his own identity, so why not over his relationships.

She would fight Dean Fawcette with any weapon she could muster but, if she was to beat him at his own game, she must never again allow him close to her, even less to kiss her.

Alice duly presented herself for tea at Creagbowie on Monday afternoon. From the beginning it was clear to Sheana there was an immediate rapport between the two older women. She was pleased Aunt Ellie had found someone of her own generation and intelligence to pass the afternoon.

Alice explained her connection with Dean's grandparents, her schoolgirl friendship with his mother and their visit to Fingaeli one summer long ago, the death of Dean's parents, the move to London and the growth of the company.

'But now I have a yearning to return to Scotland, to buy a country cottage and enjoy my twilight years.' Alice smiled. 'My parents came from near Peebles so I hadn't thought of looking in this area until Dean suggested it. He's a dear boy . . .' She sighed. 'I must admit it would be comforting to know there was someone near if ever I needed help and he is so utterly reliable.'

Sheana, overhearing the latter part of this conversation raised a sceptical eyebrow, but both Aunt Ellie and Alice Pringle were too engrossed in reminiscing to notice her. Aunt Ellie volunteered to drive Alice to view some of the properties for sale.

'We might have lunch out if you'll be free to give Tommy his, Sheana?'

'Of course I will, Aunt Ellie. It's time you enjoyed some time to yourself.' Alice Pringle looked up at her with a smile.

'Then perhaps you would all come and have lunch with me while I'm at Fingaeli. I love cooking, but there's rarely anyone to appreciate my efforts.'

'We'd love to do that, wouldn't we Sheana, and it would be good for Tommy.'

'Oh yes, please!' Tommy said with a display of enthusiasm Sheana had never seen since the accident. She knew she couldn't refuse and disappoint her young brother, but she could make sure it was not while Dean Fawcette was in residence at Fingaeli.

'That's very kind of you, Miss Pringle, so long as it's before the weekend?'

'If we went for our drive on Thursday, Ellie, perhaps I could shop for provisions in Dumfries? Then I'll cook lunch for all of us on Friday, or an evening meal if you prefer, Sheana?'

'An evening meal would suit me better.' Sheana nodded, thinking of all the tasks she needed to do. 'Thank you.'

'Yippee!' Tommy laughed with delight. 'Then Aunt Ellie can show me all the ghosts and where she used to play when she was wee like me.'

'Oh dear . . .' Alice murmured in embarrassment. Later she explained to Alice that she had kept Tommy entertained with stories she had made up about Fingaeli when he was in hospital.

'Well it is a house with a lot of character. I'm sure Tommy will find lots of interest in the nooks and crannies.'

The day after Alice Pringle's visit, Sheana received a telephone call from Mike Bain at the planning department.

'I've only just heard the good news,' he said jubilantly. 'The boss received the letter before the weekend, but I've been out of the office.'

'What good news?' Sheana asked warily.

'A-ah, then you haven't received a letter yet? The objections to the caravan park have been unconditionally withdrawn. It means you can go ahead straight away! Isn't that splendid, Sheana? I'm so pleased.'

'Are—are you sure, Mike?' Sheana asked faintly, unable to take it in, or to believe she would be spared the ordeal of the appeal.

'I'm certain. I've a copy in front of me.'

When Aunt Ellie called for Alice on Thursday one of the first things she mentioned was the withdrawal of the objections.

'Sheana is overjoyed,' she related with satisfaction. 'She's worked so hard to make things right for Tommy.'

'I'm sure she has,' Alice murmured. 'She seems to be a caring young woman—maybe like yourself . . . ?' She glanced at Ellie.

'Oh I don't know. It was no hardship to care for my brother's little family once my own chance of a happy and fulfilling life had gone. It's quite different in Sheana's case. She gave up her job and broke off a long-term relationship. She said he simply didn't understand her priorities.'

'In that case perhaps she's better without him,' Alice said firmly.

'Maybe,' Aunt Ellie acknowledged. 'I suppose you had nothing to do with Dean Fawcette withdrawing his objections, Alice?'

'He made the decision before I came up here. He's very much his own person.' Alice saw this was the ideal opportunity to mention Dean's plans for an alternative road. She had enjoyed her last visit with Ellie Lyon so much she had forgotten about the road. She proceeded to deliver bits of information.

'Even as a small boy he was always looking for challenges and solving problems,' she said with affection when she knew the seeds had been sown.

Aunt Ellie was silent while she digested the idea and concentrated on negotiating a road junction.

'I suppose it would have been a possibility,' she mused. 'If we had the money to carry it out. In fact it would have been much better for us at Creagbowie too.' She sighed. 'It always comes back to money.'

Tactfully Alice changed the subject, knowing the idea would be passed to Sheana. She had already telephoned to tell Dean of her plans for the week and how much she was enjoying Ellie's company. She was almost certain he would make it his business to arrive at Fingaeli by Friday afternoon.

CHAPTER SIXTEEN

Tommy's excitement was infectious. Aunt Ellie had dressed him up in a new sunshine yellow sweatshirt with his favourite cartoon character on the front, and long brown trousers which hid his callipers.

'Aunt Ellie's putting on her dress, the one made of shiny blue stuff,' he informed Sheana. 'Will you wear your yellow dress and look like me?'

'It's a bit summery for this weather . . .'

'Please Sheana . . . ? Then we'll both be like sunshine.' He looked up at her, his brown eye full of love. He patted his yellow chest. Sheana hugged him, swallowing the lump in her throat with an effort. She prayed every day that he would soon be walking and running around like other boys as the surgeons had forecast.

'All right, sweetheart. I'll put it on just for you. I suppose I can always take the new stole Aunt Ellie bought me for Christmas in case

Fingaeli is a bit chilly.'

There was a delicious smell of cooking wafting from the kitchen when Alice Pringle opened the door to welcome her visitors. She had thoroughly enjoyed the afternoon preparing a meal and making some of the vegetables into special shapes to tempt Tommy, as well as a raspberry mousse which had set in an old-fashioned mould she had discovered on the top shelf of one of the cupboards.

'I thought we would eat in the small parlour instead of the dining-room,' she said, leading the way.

'It's still a big room,' Aunt Ellie laughed, looking at the two long settees on either side of the fireplace as well as two Victorian tub chairs set farther back. At the far end a dining table had been set in the bay window overlooking the garden.

Alice Pringle settled them all with a drink. 'If you'll excuse me I'll just go and check the oven and bring another place setting. Dean thought I might be feeling quiet here on my own so he got away from London a bit earlier than usual. He's just taking a quick shower, but he'll be down in a minute.' Her tone was so matter of fact, so casual, but Sheana's heart had begun to thump.

She wanted to run. She hovered beside the settee, unable to bring herself to take a seat. What excuse could she make? She heard

Alice's voice, then a deeper voice. The door opened and Dean paused, his eyes widening in appreciation as his gaze rested on Sheana's slender figure in the lemon silk dress with the wide square neck and tiny sleeves.

'Why hello, Sheana,' he said easily. 'It's a pleasure to see you again.' He moved on, 'And you too Miss Lyon,' he nodded towards Aunt Ellie, smiling his charming smile and it was only as he moved to Tommy that Sheana realised she had been holding her breath. She expelled it slowly but her heart still continued thumping loudly, or so she imagined.

It was with genuine warmth and pleasure that Dean greeted Tommy, admiring his yellow sweatshirt when Tommy pointed to it.

'Aunt Ellie says I'm her wee ray of sunshine. But Sheana's a ray of sunshine too, isn't she Mr . . . er Mr . . .'

'I'm Dean. Just call me Dean, Tommy. Mister makes me feel like an old, old man.' He grinned at Tommy, but over his head he caught Sheana's eyes on him and inclined his head. He guessed she was blaming him for Tommy's confusion over his name. He gave a wry grimace, acknowledging his own foolishness.

The meal was delicious and leisurely. When it was over Dean lifted Tommy from his seat and carried him to one of the settees, settling him comfortably with a cushion beneath his head, before he sat down beside him. He

122

began to ask Alice how she had spent her week at Fingaeli and as they talked his long fingers gently stroked Tommy's temple and the dark curls at his brow. In no time at all the little boy was sound asleep.

'He was so excited about coming here tonight,' Aunt Ellie said, 'and he ate such a good meal, no wonder he's sleepy. Perhaps we should take him home now.'

'Yes we should,' Sheana said quickly, too quickly.

'Don't go yet, Miss Lyon. Tommy will be fine and I'm sure Alice still has lots to tell you. Anyway I'd like Sheana's advice about Fingaeli's back premises before you leave.'

He turned to Sheana. 'Shall we go?' he asked pleasantly. There was no way she could refuse without causing a fuss. Dean lifted her fine woollen stole from the back of a chair. 'We'll take this with us. There's no heating in the servants' quarters and you may feel the cold.'

As soon as the door was closed Sheana turned to him. 'There's no need to—to . . .'

'Yes? To what . . .' Dean's eyes were full of laughter and she stared at him. 'No need for me to apologise because I kissed you the last time we met?'

'No! I—I mean there's . . .'

'Good. Because I've no intention of apologising for doing something I enjoyed.' His eyes held hers and she felt the colour staining her cheeks. She felt as gauche as a young schoolgirl.

'Come,' Dean said gently, 'I really would like your advice. I'm considering converting some of the back premises into a self-contained flat for Alice, unless she sees a cottage she would prefer.'

'Aunt Ellie would love that,' Sheana said before she had time to consider. 'I—I mean they seem to get on so well, and in such a short time. It's as though they've known each other for ages . . .'

'Yes, that's the impression I got from Alice. This week away will have done her a world of good. We had rather a sad business within the company. Alice takes these things to heart. She feels responsible for other people, you see.'

'Oh. I didn't know.'

'No, it's better she should put it behind her now. We've done all that can be done and I'm selling the company as soon as arrangements can be made for the take over. Alice will retire and I shall move to Fingaeli.'

'I—I see. I er . . . I suppose I should thank you for withdrawing your objections to the caravan park,' she stammered reluctantly.

'You shouldn't thank me unless you mean it,' he said with an ironic quirk of one dark brow.

'Oh, but I do! It will mean everything to Tommy if we can stay at Creagbowie and make a living. I—that is Aunt Ellie told me about your idea to make an alternative route and protect Fingaeli's peace and quiet. I—I would have considered it, but we simply can't afford anything as major as that, at least not for several years.'

'My dear girl, no-one would expect you to foot the bill for a new road when the benefits are mainly for Fingaeli . . .' He shepherded her through a door at the end of the passage causing her to shiver in the sudden chill air.

Immediately he unfolded her stole and placed it around her shoulders, but instead of leaving it at that he turned her towards him and pulled it closer.

'Sheana, if you really would be willing to sacrifice a strip of your field—the one which leads from the back road to the shore—I would be really grateful. Your solicitor will be quick to realise an alternative entrance would be increasing the amenity value of Fingaeli of course, so he would see you were not out of pocket.'

'B—but . . .' Sheana stared up at him. 'It would cost an awful lot of money . . .'

'Your land, my money.' He shrugged. 'I think it would be a fair deal, but I admit it would be a tremendous benefit to me, so it's one I wouldn't mind paying for. If you consider it go and see your solicitor and let me know.'

He knew better than to persist. Sheana had

a mind of her own. 'Now, come and look at these rooms and give me your opinion on how to convert them into a comfortable ground floor flat with a nice garden.'

He moved her forward but he still kept an arm lightly around her shoulders and Sheana found she didn't mind at all. Indeed she enjoyed the feeling of being protected and sheltered and her feeling of warmth came from within as much as from her cashmere stole.

'This would make a lovely sitting-room,' she said, 'especially if this window could be made to reach the floor so that Miss Pringle could step out into her garden. It's sheltered from view and from the wind by the back of the old stables, and it gets the morning and afternoon sun.'

'A-ah now I hadn't considered that,' Dean admitted as he paced across the room making a rough measurement. They explored the other empty rooms, enjoying sparking ideas off each other. Eventually Dean led her along a short passage and out into the grounds.

'This would make a lovely little garden,' Sheana said, turning towards him enthusiastically, not realising he was so close behind her.

'Heavenly,' he murmured, steadying her, but keeping her close against his chest. 'Your ideas have been invaluable,' he murmured gruffly and his arms tightened, drawing her even closer. Sheana felt small and defenceless, and very safe.

Dean lowered his head and kissed her mouth—a light kiss. She felt a pang of disappointment. But he was looking deep into her eyes as though searching her soul. Her breath came faster . . .

'Oh Dean . . .' It was no more than a whisper, but it was enough. This time his kiss was even more satisfying than the one which had haunted her dreams.

It was a long time before Dean held her gently away from him and looked down into her rosy face and shining eyes. His voice was husky with emotion.

'This may have been unplanned, my darling Sheana, but I know it's going to be the most wonderful development of my life.'